THIS SIDE OF HELL

Corporal David Canning buried his best friend below the burning African sand. Then he was alone, with a bullet-sprayed ambulance containing five seriously injured men and one hysterical nurse in his care. He faced heat, dust, thirst and hunger; and somewhere in the area roamed almost two hundred blood-crazed tribesmen led by a white mercenary with his own desperate reasons for catching up with the sole survivors of the massacre. But Canning vowed that he would win through to safety.

LP C

3/14

A
a
i

ROBERT CHARLES

THIS SIDE OF HELL

Complete and Unabridged

00305293579

LINFORD
Leicester

First published in Great Britain

First Linford Edition
published 1999

British Library CIP Data

Charles, Robert, *1938* –
    This side of hell.—Large print ed.—
    Linford mystery library
    1. Detective and mystery stories
    2. Large type books
    I. Title
    823.9′14 [F]

    ISBN 0–7089–5456–1

Published by
F. A. Thorpe (Publishing) Ltd.
Anstey, Leicestershire
Set by Words & Graphics Ltd.
Anstey, Leicestershire
Printed and bound in Great Britain by
T. J. International Ltd., Padstow, Cornwall

This book is printed on acid-free paper

Daybreak at Sakinda

The sun came up from the hills behind
Sakinda; a scarlet disc that bathed the
eastern skyline with blood, as though
grimly symbolising the events that were
to come. Yet at the moment not one of
the small detachment of British soldiers
waiting in the dusty clearing between
the clusters of mud and wattle huts that
made up the village had any premonition
of impending disaster. The heat was not
yet strong enough to drive them into the
shade of their vehicles or the round,
thatch-roofed huts, and they lounged idly
in the open.

Lieutenant James Holland, the officer
in charge, gazed around the encampment
with a feeling of satisfaction. He was
young and inexperienced, and this was
his first tour of duty outside the barrack
squares of England, but the feeling of
doing a real job of soldiering at last gave
him a sense of fulfilment that helped

to boost his confidence. The morale of the men was high, and he knew that Hardman, his sergeant, possessed all the practical experience that he lacked. With that kind of support he felt that he could not fail to do a good job.

He glanced at the limp, dust-stained flag of the United Nations that was securely lashed to the windscreen upright of his open jeep, and he felt proud to be serving under their command. The thankless task of keeping the peace, such as the United Nations were doing now in this breakaway Congo state of Katanga, was, in his opinion, the only true job for a soldier in these present times. Holland had always been something of an idealist as well as an army officer, and now that he had been in Africa long enough to witness some of the misery caused by the greedy squabbling of the power-hungry politicians he was convinced that his opinions were right.

His gaze travelled past the jeep, registering the details of the village and compound in his orderly mind. Most of the native population of Sakinda had made themselves scarce, but a few of the tribesmen watched them from between the huts with wary, slightly hostile eyes. The only woman in sight was a wrinkled old crone, wrapped in a shapeless dress of faded cotton cloth, who squatted on her heels before one of the huts and stared with seemingly sightless eyes into the cooking pot before her.

Holland knew that the village was not really hostile. It was just that tomorrow the white soldiers would be gone, and they would again be at the mercy of marauding terrorists. And with the whole of the Belgian Congo simmering in a blood bath it was not prudent to risk the anger of one party by offering open friendship to the other.

Beyond the limits of the village tiny grey monkeys darted to and fro, chattering wildly in the higher branches of the trees. The jungle was broken by patches of thorn-bush, and to the north stretched an open plain of low brush and savannah grassland, dotted with clumps of flat-topped trees. To the east the sun had now lifted higher above the forested hills, and the sky had mellowed to a pale crimson.

Holland's gaze came back to the compound, ranging over the four trucks that provided transport for the forty-two men under his command. Behind the last truck stood a large field ambulance, and by the cab the driver, a strongly built young corporal, and his mate were talking idly. Holland frowned as he saw the ambulance.

Yesterday, the day his detachment had arrived at Sakinda, one of the men had suddenly fallen sick with an unexplained fever. Holland had radioed for medical help, but unfortunately the helicopters normally used in such an emergency had all been fully occupied, and as the sick man's condition was not considered too serious the ambulance had been sent instead. Holland had been forced to wait while the ambulance made the six hour trip from Kasuvu in the south where it had been stationed. And now he had received reports from the village headman which indicated terrorist movements near the Kasuvu road and obliged him to

4

provide the ambulance with an escort for at least part of the journey back. To Holland the delay was infuriating.

Holland's present job was to locate and, if possible, capture a white mercenary who was reported to be leading a terrorist band of Bantu warriors somewhere in the jungles beyond that savannah plain to the north of Sakinda. The mercenary was one of the many renegade whites fighting for the breakaway government of Katanga. The state of Katanga covered some of the richest copper belts in the Congo, and could well afford to pay the grim-faced soldiers of fortune who led its tattered native soldiery.

Holland had heard gruesome rumours of two elderly Belgian priests working in a lonely jungle mission who had been butchered by the Bantu under this mercenary's command, and he was savagely eager to get to grips with his quarry. His idealistic mind couldn't quite comprehend the mentality of a man who could be a partner to such a crime. The Bantu he could understand. They were frightened, and frightened primitives surrounded by starvation, misery and warfare could hardly be expected to react other than violently. Violence was an instinctive reaction of self defence, and it was unfortunate that ignorance prevented them from separating friend form foe. But the white mercenary! The *civilised* white man! There Holland's understanding trailed off into genuine bewilderment.

There were rumours that said the mercenary was a tough, ex N.C.O. who had deserted from the French Foreign Legion. There were rumours that said he was a giant red-bearded Russian, and a fanatical Communist. There were rumours that said he was a scar-faced South African from the Transvaal, and rumours that said he was an Englishman with a public school accent. Perhaps there were men who vaguely fitted all these conflicting descriptions among the many mercenaries fighting for Katanga, and perhaps this particular man was someone totally different. Holland did not know, but he had an almost ghoulish desire to find out. He wanted to look his quarry in the face and find out just how evil the man really looked.

Holland wanted to be heading north. He did not want to turn south again to escort an ambulance just because some snivelling private had gone down with some silly, blasted bug.

He glared angrily at the ambulance, and then he noticed a movement from the small army tent that had been pitched just behind it. His scowl cleared and his anger began to fade as he watched the tent flap open.

A young woman in the uniform of a Lieutenant Nurse stepped out of the tent. She straightened up and arched her shoulders back in a grateful stretching gesture that thrust her breasts hard against her khaki blouse and emphasised that there was a neatly curved figure beneath the concealing uniform. She looked around the compound, inclined her head in a brief nod of greeting to the two men by the ambulance, and then she saw Holland watching her. She smiled warmly and made her way towards him.

Holland watched her approach and

decided that there was the silver lining in his patricular cloud. If the ambulance had not arrived, then Nurse Rona Waring would not have arrived either. And he would not have enjoyed the most pleasant evening of his life the previous night.

She stopped in front of him.

'Good morning, Lieutenant.'

'Good morning, Miss Waring.' Holland possessed a boyish smile coupled with clean, smooth features and sharp blue eyes that many woman found attractive, and he made full use of them now. For the previous night had made him confident that Rona Waring was one of those many women. 'What do you think of Sakinda by daylight?' he asked.

She glanced at her surroundings and smiled. 'Apart from the heat, and the dust, and the flies, I'd say it was charmingly attractive. I almost wish I could stay.'

Holland realised that more than half his men were listening to every word they were saying, and reluctantly he turned the conversation back to a more business-like foundation.

'How is Private Garner this morning?'

Her smile vanished. 'He's very sick. I'd like to get him back to that little hospital at Kasuvu as quickly as possible.'

'We are ready to move out as soon as you are. But perhaps we'd better take a look at him first.'

The nurse nodded and together they walked over to the ambulance.

Corporal David Canning, the ambulance driver, saw them coming and anticipated their intentions. He moved to the back of his vehicle and opened the doors so that they could climb inside. Holland offered him a brief, 'good morning,' but the nurse did not speak. Canning wondered whether her toffee nose would eventually melt in the sun.

Holland looked down at the sweating, stubble-masked face of the sick man lying on the lower of the two left hand side bunks. Garner's condition had worsened considerably since Holland had first radioed for help late the previous afternoon. The ambulance had arrived at nightfall, and Garner had been immediately made comfortable in the

9

back. But the darkness and the terrorist reports that had come from Sakinda's headman soon after the ambulance had arrived had forced Holland to order a delay until dawn before the vehicle started on its return journey.

Rona Waring laid a slim hand upon Garner's temple and the man squirmed under her touch. She looked at Holland with worried eyes.

'He's very bad. The fever's taken an even stronger grip on him during the night.'

'All right, I'll tell the Sergeant to get the men moving.'

She straightened up. 'Are you sure that's really necessary. After all, we got here safely without an escort. And those big red crosses are big enough to see. Surely they wouldn't attack an ambulance?'

Holland hesitated. He badly wanted to start moving north and get on with the search. And he had a slightly guilty feeling that if Rona Waring had not been aboard the ambulance he probably would have allowed it to go without an escort.

Then he remembered the two murdered priests, and he knew that despite the nurse's belief to the contrary those big red crosses would provide no protection whatsoever if the ambulance were to run into one of the roaming terrorist bands. He said slowly.

'I think I'd better come with you for the first half of the way at least. I'd rather waste a few hours now than spend the rest of my life regretting it.'

She accepted his decision. 'I'll ride in the ambulance,' she said. 'There's not much that I can do for him, except hold him still if he becomes too feverish.'

He frowned. 'You sat up with him all night after you left me. Are you sure you don't want some help?'

She smiled. 'I can manage. It's my job.'

He nodded, and then turned away. He dropped down on to the dusty ground outside the ambulance and glanced around the compound.

'Hardman!' he shouted. 'Sergeant Hardman.'

Hardman appeared almost immediately

from behind one of the stationary lorries. He was a solid bull of a man with a jaw-line that looked to be two or three sizes too large for the rest of his blunt face. His sixteen and a half stone made an impressive filling for his outsize uniform, and apart from a slight paunch he didn't carry an ounce of surplus fat. It was impossible to picture him as anything but a regular army sergeant.

'Sir!' he barked.

Holland said briskly. 'Get the men moving, Sergeant. Two lorries and half the men will stay here with the reserves of petrol and our supplies. The other two lorries and the remainder of the men will form an escort for the ambulance back to Kasuvu. You will come with me and the escort. Sergeant Riley will be in command here until we get back.'

Riley, an older, but equally capable N.C.O., had stepped up beside Hardman. He saluted in acknowledgement.

Hardman barked another ringing, 'Sir!' And then spun round to bellow out a stream of orders.

On the far side of the compound

Private Mike Delayney reached wearily for his rifle, his face creasing with disgust.

'There goes Sergeant-bloody-Hardman — living up to his bloody name again.'

Ginger Morris, a red-haired shrimp of a man who always looked to be just on the point of falling out of his unbuttoned battle blouse, simply grinned and said quickly.

'I'll tell you what, Irish. I'll lay you half a ton of codswallop to a can of cold shamrocks that there's at least one blank space on our dear Sergeant's birth certificate.'

'And I'd bet that there are two,' Delayney grinned back.

'I don't think he had a mother either.'

Hardman roared again and their grins faded.

'I wonder what he'd look like with his face kicked in,' Delayney muttered sourly.

Both men moved to obey the Sergeant's orders.

By the first of the waiting lorries a tall, rangy man named Baxter sat in the dust with his back against the front wheel. He had been practising a few soft, low notes on a small, but well made harmonica which he played quietly to himself. He was quite good, although most of his mates flatly refused to admit it, and now there were a few good-natured murmurs of approval as he replaced the harmonica in its box and slipped the box back into the top pocket of his blouse. Baxter smiled, mostly to himself, and stood up, reaching for his rifle.

Private Jack Foster, a married man in his late thirties, reluctantly folded up the last letter he had received from his wife and pushed it back into its envelope. The letter had reached him only two days before and he had already read it eleven times. There was nothing in it except vague comments on the weather and the two kids, and some barely readable gossip about Mrs. Johns next door, but it was from his Rose, and that alone made it something special. He scowled at Hardman, whom he believed he hated and picked up his rifle.

In a remarkably short space of time Hardman had the men detailed for escort duty aboard the first two lorries each man armed with either a rifle or a sten gun. He knew that half of them hated his guts and that the other half disliked him intensely. But that didn't matter. It was a sergeant's job to be hated. The warm hope that the sergeant would fall flat on his face in the mud, or else get a bullet up his backside, was one of the things that kept the men going when things got rough.

Hardman reported to Holland that the convoy was ready to move out.

David Canning observed some of the resentful glares that were directed at Hardman's back and wondered which was worse — taking orders from an ignorant bull like Hardman, or from an oily-smiled woman like Lieutenant Nurse Waring. He glanced at his mate, Roy Spencer, leaning against the ambulance cab beside him, and said suddenly:

'Well at least we don't have to have her sitting up front with us this trip. That other poor blighter's stuck with her in the back.' He jerked a thumb at the ambulance behind him as he spoke.

Spencer looked at him, slightly amused. He was a thin, dark youth, lively and quick moving.

'I rather enjoyed having her sit between us,' he said. 'I was almost tempted to faint in her lap.'

'She would have squirmed like hell and had you on a court martial for touching an officer, even if the faint had been genuine.'

Spencer eyed the strong-boned, but slightly sullen face of his partner. 'Corp, I think you're a woman hater,' he said.

Canning grinned, and with the sullenness wiped away he had the eyes and smile of a rogue. He was not very tall, about five foot seven or eight, but he was stockily built.

'Not women,' he said. 'Just officers. There's a difference.'

But even as he said it he knew that it was not that reason alone that made him resent Rona Waring. The Lieutenant Nurse with her fair hair and baby blue eyes reminded him too much of Jenny. He stamped on the thought angrily and changed the subject.

'They'll be pulling off any second. Let's get in the cab.'

Spencer nodded, and together they climbed into their respective seats. Spencer picked up his sten gun from the floor of the cab and settled it on his knees. Canning made himself comfortable behind the wheel and leaned his own sten against his seat. From the open communication panel behind Canning's head Rona Waring said quietly.

'Take it easy as possible over the bumps, Corporal. He is sleeping quietly at the moment.'

Spencer smiled. 'Yes, Ma'am.'

Canning merely nodded.

Holland was already in his jeep, talking to Hardman who stood beside him.

'I'll lead the way, Sergeant. You will follow with the first lorry, then the ambulance, and the second lorry can bring up the rear. If we pass any natives I'll stop and find out what I can about these terrorists that are supposed to be in the area. I'm pretty sure most of them are to the north, not the south, but I can't ignore the headman's warning.'

'Very good, sir.'

Hardman saluted, walked back to pass on instructions to both Canning and the driver of the second lorry, and then he swung into the cab beside the driver of the first vehicle.

Holland's jeep moved off along the dusty Kasuvu road. The rest of the convoy followed.

The men left behind began to relax.

★ ★ ★

Twenty-five miles to the south, just a bare mile away from the Kasuvu road, was a large clearing in jungle. Here, moving restlessly and chattering among themselves, swarmed a horde of nearly two hundred Bantu warriors. They were armed with a vast assortment of bows and arrows, spears, knives, clubs, ancient shotguns, and modern fully automatic rifles. Those with the more primitive weapons hungrily tested the cutting edges of their spears and knives, while those fortunate enough to have been supplied with rifles from

Katanga's armoury fondled the shining steel and polished gun stocks with eager, half reverent hands.

In the centre of the clearing a lone white man crouched before a patch of cleared earth and drew a map on the ground with the point of a knife.

He was neither Russian nor South African. He had never been a Communist and he had never been a Legionaire. And he had never been inside an English public school. In fact all the rumours had been wrong.

The man was a Belgian. His name was Larocque.

At the moment he was being closely watched by Mambiro, the headman of the Bantu horde, and all of the leading warriors. The map he had drawn detailed the surrounding area, and especially the Kasuvu road.

Larocque said calmly.

'The runner who came from Sakinda during the night has told us that the white soldiers will be coming down this road in their trucks. It will take them three hours to reach this river crossing, here. It is a perfect stopping place and it is almost certain that their chief will call a halt so that they can rest. They will get down from their trucks and that is when we will take them by surprise and attack.'

Larocque's command of the Bantu language was good, but still Mambiro repeated the words to make sure that his men understood. He finished by saying grimly.

'We will kill them all.'

Larocque raised his hand. 'No,' he said. 'Not all.'

Mambiro flashed him a glare that was full of suspicion. The other warriors stiffened, their black hands closing faster round their shiny new rifles.

Larocque sensed that the situation could turn nasty in an instant, but his hard, darkly-bronzed face showed no sign as he reached slowly into the breast pocket of his bush shirt. He drew out a slightly creased, postcard-sized photograph showing the head and shoulders of a man in British Army uniform. He held the photograph out to Mambiro.

'All but this man,' he said quietly. 'I want to talk to this man. I want him alive.'

Mambiro stared at the picture.

'He should die,' he snarled. 'He is an enemy of Katanga. They should all die.'

Larocque smiled. 'I agree. But I want to talk to this man before he dies. Does it matter if one death is delayed for a few hours.'

The smile won response.

'You will lead us to victory. I will show this picture to my warriors and tell them that we want this man alive,' Mambiro promised.

Larocque stood up and laid his hand upon the headman's shoulder.

'It is agreed,' he said solemnly. 'It is a bargain.'

Ambush

The Sakinda-Kasuvu road was nothing more than a narrow, rutted track disappearing into the heart of the Central African bush. In places it was only wide enough to give comfortable passage to a jeep or a Land Rover, and the two heavy lorries and the ambulance were constantly scraped and battered by tangles of thornbush and overhanging branches as they practically bulldozed their way through. The four vehicles of the convoy bumped and jolted alarmingly over the bumps and gullies, their engines roaring and their wheels spinning up a great white fog of dust clouds as they churned onwards.

In the driving seat of the ambulance David Canning was silently cursing the young Lieutenant who had insisted on providing them with an escort. The drive up to Sakinda had been bad enough, but now, with the lorry and the jeep ahead throwing up smothering dust clouds and making it necessary to have every window fully closed in order to breathe, the heat was fast becoming unbearable. They had already covered several miles and the sun was now a merciless glare that dominated the whole blue waste of the sky.

Somehow, despite the closed windows, the fine dust was penetrating into the vehicle and settling in a choking, powdery film. The whole cab was an oven of dust and heat, and the ever strengthening smell of sweat. The back of Canning's shirt was already sticking to his shoulders and when he glanced at Spencer he could see the moisture glistening on his friend's face. He wondered how the nurse behind them was reacting to the smell, and he was almost tempted to smile. He had already decided that Lieutenant Nurse Waring was the kind of fancy female who would be slightly disgusted by the scent of human sweat, and he could picture her pretty nose wrinkling with distaste. The thought was his only comfort.

Canning resented the nurse even more than he cursed Holland, for he was convinced that it was only her presence that had induced the young officer to provide them with this unwanted escort. He and Spencer were both armed with stens and he felt that they were quite capable of scaring off a few natives if any should appear. Holland's concern was just an excuse to impress the girl.

The front off-side wheel of the ambulance slipped suddenly into a deep gulley. The vehicle lurched with a wild swaying movement and Canning barely checked a vicious, purely-masculine oath as the steering wheel strained and pulled in his hands. The front wheel rose and then, seconds later, the ambulance gave another crazy sway as the rear wheel dipped into the same gulley. Canning kept his mouth tightly shut. For the first time in an hour Roy Spencer's face almost relaxed into a smile of sympathy. Canning went back to his brooding.

The convoy snarled its way onwards through the bush, leaving a swirling river of dust in its wake. A troop of gibbering baboons chattered an angry protest at the disturbance from the upper branches of two tall baobabs, and a herd of startled antelope fled like flashes of brown quicksilver from the noise. A large puff adder uncoiled itself with a quivering hiss and slithered swiftly from the track to the safety of the bush. The sun blazed a climbing pathway across the empty sky.

In the leading jeep Holland sat upright and alert beside his sweating driver, his eyes slitted against the glare of heat but conscientiously probing every new bend and twist of the road as it came into view. He wasn't expecting trouble, but it was his job to be prepared.

In the back of the following lorry Mike Delayney was moodily reminiscing over the shape, charm, and co-operative abilities of a far-off North London barmaid. His mates listened without comment. The heat and dust were too wearying for even Delayney's detailed and colourful memories to excite any enthusiasm.

In the last lorry Baxter was sitting slightly apart from his companions, leaning forward with his elbows balanced on his kness and again playing softly on his harmonica. The tune was 'Summertime,' but Baxter's face was expressionless, and any irony he may have intended was lost upon the silently suffering men around him.

The ambulance in the centre of the convoy lurched into yet another unexpected gully, and this time Canning was too late to check the violent oath that was his immediate reaction. The outburst drew a quick, infectious grin from Spencer, and Canning relaxed a fraction and smiled back. Neither dared turn their heads to look at the nurse and they continued to stare solemnly ahead. Canning wondered whether she was blushing, and felt highly satisfied with the crudity of the phrase he had used.

Rona Waring was in fact colouring slightly, but the red flush in her cheeks was more due to anger than to maidenly modesty. After two years of army nursing she had heard most of the barrack room expressions, and perhaps this one more than most, but usually the man concerned would have the grace to make some sort of apology afterwards. Now this sour-faced Corporal was simply ignoring her, as though he didn't know that she must have overheard.

However, before she had time to shape a suitably sharp retort to remind him of her presence the sick private on the bed began to twist in a sudden spasm of fevered movement. For the next few minutes she was kept busy holding the sweating man still, her anxiety over his temperature and condition pushing the Corporal's rudeness from her mind.

★ ★ ★

Two hours later Canning saw the driver of the lorry ahead give a weary signal to slow down, and he equally wearily lowered his own window to pass the signal on. Above the noise of the engines he could hear Holland's voice ordering a halt, and then the roaring bellow of Hardman making the order doubly clear. The leading lorry rolled to a stop and Canning brought the ambulance to a standstill just behind it. He switched off his engine and heaved a sigh of relief as he arched his aching shoulder muscles before relaxing.

'Thank Christ for that,' he said. 'I thought he was going to go on for ever.'

Spencer released a sigh of his own. 'It's not before time,' he conceded.

There was sweet silence for a moment now that the roaring of the engines had stopped, and then the burly figure of Hardman appeared, walking back down the length of the convoy. His shirt sleeves were rolled up to reveal monstrously hairy forearms, but the three sergeant's stripes were still clearly visible. His bawling voice echoed like that of an angry bull as he passed on Holland's orders.

'Everybody out of the lorries. You've got fifteen minutes for a breather and a smoke, stretch your legs and shake hands with your best friend. And don't lose yourselves in the ruddy bushes doing it!'

Canning smiled. It had obviously slipped Hardman's mind that there was a woman in the ambulance, and he wondered how the Lieutenant Nurse was taking that little turn of army phraseology.

Then Rona Waring spoke from directly behind him.

'Corporal, would either you or your mate please come round the back and watch over the patient for five minutes.'

Canning hesitated, but Spencer quickly answered for him.

'I'll come round Ma'am. Take as long as you like.'

Canning said briefly, 'thanks Roy.' And turning his back on the nurse he opened his cab door and swung down to the ground.

A flush flared in Rona Waring's cheeks. She had both seen and understood the derisive smile that had flitted across Canning's face a few moments ago, and his unrepentant oath when the ambulance had crashed through the gulley was still fresh in her mind. She decided abruptly that the Corporal was carrying his insolence just a little too far.

Spencer appeared to pull open the back doors of the ambulance and the nurse gave him a brief, icy nod as he climbed in to take her place. She dropped down into the dust and moved round to the front of the vehicle to find Canning leaning slackly against the cab. His back was towards her and his right hand was fishing into the breast pocket of his shirt as he reached for his cigarettes.

She said sharply.

'Corporal!'

Canning turned, and common sense made him straighten himself up as she advanced towards him. She was a good three inches shorter than he, and at that moment her blue eyes were cold and angry. Canning's mouth tightened as he realised again how similar she looked to Jenny. Put them together and they could pass for twin sisters. And Jenny had been a tramp. For a moment it seemed crazy to believe that he had once wanted to marry a woman like that.

She said curtly.

'I don't know what kind of a chip you've got on your shoulder, Corporal, but I suggest that you get rid of it before it costs you your stripes. And kindly keep your language under control the next time the ambulance hits a little bump. I'm not a prude, but neither am I accustomed to hearing the filthy expression you choose to use.'

The entire reprimand was scathing, but there was something in the intonation of that one word Corporal that made Canning shut his mouth even tighter. He couldn't trust himself to speak.

Rona Waring glared into his set face and resisted a sudden temptation to slap the palm of her hand hard across his mouth. Instead she said.

'Go back and relieve your mate. That's an order!'

Canning knew it was an unnecessary order, for it was barely two minutes since Spencer had taken her place in the ambulance. She simply wanted to demonstrate her authority; to rub in the fact that she was a Lieutenant while he was only a Corporal. He swallowed his pride and saluted slowly.

'Yes, Ma'am.'

Then he turned towards the back of the ambulance.

Rona Waring hesitated as he moved away, but she held her temper with an effort and strode briskly towards the front of the convoy. She told herself grimly that even though she didn't want any unpleasantness she would at least have a new driver before she left Kasuvu again.

Spencer was grinning as Canning climbed into the back of the ambulance.

'Did I hear you get a rollicking, Corp?' he asked.

With another man Canning might have exploded, but there was something so completely inoffensive about Spencer's grin that Canning unexpectedly found himself smiling back.

'Something like that,' he said.

Spencer straightened his back.

'Where's she gone now then?'

'To associate with her own class no doubt, holding hands with pretty-boy Holland.' His voice turned sour again as he added. 'Not that he'll have much luck. I'll bet she doesn't sleep with anything under the rank of Major.'

At the head of the convoy Holland was

standing by his jeep and methodically
making a mental note of his surroundings.
Directly ahead a small, shallow stream
cut a path squarely across the dirt road
that led to Kasuvu. In wet weather it
would be impassable, a roaring torrent
of almost liquid mud tearing its way
through the bush, but now it offered no
problem and could be forded easily. On
either side of the road the ground was
fairly clear but for low thorn-bush and
scrub, the bushes gradually gaining in
height and density until they merged into
a jungle background. Holland watched
his men climbing wearily out of their
trucks, grumbling and complaining among
themselves. Hardman was standing by
the last lorry with his hands on his
thighs, his eyes squinted against the heat
and glare.

Holland removed his pale blue, United
Nations beret and rubbed the sweat
from his temples with the palm of his
hand. Then he saw Rona Waring coming
towards him and quickly readjusted the
beret to its correct angle.

The nurse gave him a strained smile,

determined not to allow any sign of her recent clash with Canning to show upon her face.

Holland said cheerfully. 'Next stop Kasuvu. Don't let the heat get you down.'

'I don't doubt that it will be just as hot at Kasuvu.' She looked towards the stream and added. 'I didn't think anyone had invented water in this God-forsaken country.'

Holland gestured towards a single massive tree that had embedded its great roots deep in the soil near the stream's bank. 'Let's move over there in the shade,' he suggested. 'We've got fifteen minutes before moving on and I don't fancy standing out here in the full blast of the sun.'

Together they started to move away from the jeep, and the movement saved Holland's life. He had rested his hand lightly on Rona Waring's arm as he guided her forwards, and in the same instant an automatic rifle cracked violently on the far side of the stream. The bullet tore across the curve of the young Lieutenant's left shoulder, jerking his hand away from the girl and spinning him off balance to land face downwards in the dirt.

Simultaneously there came a roar of warning from Hardman, and then two shattering explosions. Holland's jeep reared up in the air as the first thrown grenade landed directly beneath its radiator, the luckless driver shrieking aloud as the vehicle twisted, threw him sideways, and then crashed down on top of him. The second grenade passed neatly through the cab window of the leading lorry and landed with a crippling thud square in the driver's lap. It was a freak throw and blew both the man and the interior of the cab to pieces.

David Canning jerked upright at the sound of the explosions and catapulted himself out of the ambulance. Hardman was already running up towards him, yelling at the men to get down. Then a third grenade landed beside the front wheel of the ambulance.

Hardman moved with the graceless speed of a bull rhino at the height of its charge. He left the ground in a running dive to scoop up the ugly metallic pineapple with one hand, rolling smoothly on to his back and hurling it back into the bush. It happened so fast that Canning could only stare and blink.

Then the grenade exploded in the bush and was echoed by the fourth grenade that blew up the last truck. Canning sprang into movement and sprinted towards his cab, jerking open the door and grabbing at his sten.

The whole of the surrounding bush was suddenly full of screaming Bantu tribesmen, rising upright from the low scrub where they had lain flat on their stomachs, concealed by a cunning camouflage of cut branches. Spear points flashed in the sun and the evil cracking of automatic rifles resounded in the hot dry air. Canning dropped flat and fired a chattering, sweeping burst that smashed three of the nearest tribesmen back to the earth.

Over half the men had left their weapons in the trucks, but those who had kept their arms with them fired frenziedly back into the bush. Hardman yelled at them again to get down and thrust the nearest private flat on his face. Quickly the scattered men took cover against the wrecked vehicles, but Hardman ignored his own advice and heaved himself over the back of the middle lorry. A burst of fire ripped through the canvas hood beside his head but he was moving fantastically fast for a man of his huge bulk and rolled on to the floor of the lorry unharmed. He scrambled to his knees and swiftly began hurling the stacked rifles and stens out of the back of the lorry where the unarmed men could reach them. Finally he left the lorry in a flying leap with a sten cradled in his arms, firing steadily into the mass of gleaming black bodies surging from the bush even before he hit the ground.

Holland's right shoulder was a mass of fire and there were tears of agony in his eyes as he struggled frantically to his knees. His face was white with shock and only Rona Waring, screaming his name and pulling at his shoulder to help him upright, convinced him that he was not suffering from some sudden, terrible nightmare. He heard Hardman roaring as he rallied the men, and then saw the bloodied remnants of his driver still twisting beneath the overturned jeep. Then the nurse screamed again and he became aware of a solid mass of Bantu warriors rushing through the shallow waters of the stream towards him.

Holland lurched upright and dragged the nurse close against the wrecked jeep.

'Keep your head down,' he said painfully. And then he tugged his army revolver from the leather holster at his hip and fired into the oncoming tribesmen.

He saw a black body spin and fall, threshing in the waters of the stream. Then he fired again and missed. There were too many of them and he decided without emotion that he was about to die. For one fleeting moment he wondered whether he ought to shoot the nurse first.

Then there was the sound of heavy running footsteps behind him, a blessedly familiar bull-like roar, and then the harsh stuttering of a sten gun. The Bantu war cries changed to death screams in mid-voice and the black warriors fell back.

The sten gun stopped and Hardman said crisply:

'Are you all right, Lieutenant? Sir!'

Holland's face was still white and the shoulder of his shirt was red with blood. But he could still move his arm and he knew he had only been creased. The shoulder was already growing numb.

He said weakly. 'I'm all right, Sergeant. Look after Lieutenant Waring will you.'

'Sir!' Hardman acknowledged. And wrapping one huge arm about the nurse's waist he lifted her bodily and carried her back towards the leading lorry where the bulk of the men were still keeping up a rain of defensive fire against the Bantu attacking from either side. Holland staggered after them.

For a moment there was a lull in the fighting and Holland tried desperately to clear the daze of pain from his mind. He had dropped on his knees beside the shattered cab of the lorry and Rona Waring was kneeling beside him, her fingers fumbling to pull his blood-soaked shirt from his wounded shoulder.

'Keep still, Jimmy,' she said shrilly. 'You must let me fix this.'

Holland pulled away. 'There's no time,' he said hoarsely. 'Sergeant Hardman, what's the position?'

Hardman said grimly, 'All the vehicles except the ambulance destroyed sir. Five men dead, several wounded.'

Holland looked slowly down the line of wrecked vehicles.

He said, 'Tell the radio operator to — '

'Sorry, sir!' Hardman's words seemed to be grating through his teeth. 'They had the radio operator marked down, sir. He must have been hit two or three times, and two shots smashed the transmitter.'

Holland said nothing.

Three minutes later the Bantu attacked again. The very first shot caught Hardman full in the chest.

The big Sergeant had been kneeling with his sten at the ready when the crushing impact slammed his shoulders hard against the front wheel of the lorry behind him. The sten gun fell limply beside him, still trailing from one sagging hand. He stared stupidly at the red stain spreading over his chest and rubbed his free hand almost wonderingly through the blood.

He thought stolidly; I musn't die; I'm the Sergeant; they hate my guts and that's why they'll fight to stay alive; they want to see me die, that's why I've got to stay alive and make them wait for it. The pain sent up a hazy mist to blurr his vision and he thought again; that's what keeps them going when things get rough, the hope that the Sergeant will get his first. Got to stay alive and keep them hoping.

He tried to pull the sten up to his shoulder against, just to show them all that the Sergeant was still alive, but instead it was his shoulder that fell down on to the sten, and everything went black.

Holland stared down and for the first time felt real horror as the screams of the Bantu echoed with the crackling of rifle fire across the clearing.

A Grim Decision

The second onslaught lasted for seven terribly bloody minutes. David Canning lay full length beneath the ambulance with his sten pulled hard against his shoulder, his face a strained mass of dust and sweat as he methodically covered the right-hand side of the road. Spencer lay beside him, covering the opposite side. The men from the last lorry had followed the example of the two ambulance drivers and had wriggled underneath their wrecked vehicle. Led by a lance-corporal named Harris they put up a solid defence until an accurately aimed throwing spear almost severed Harris's head from his shoulders. In the same moment Baxter shrieked with agony as a bullet shattered his left ankle. Holland had rallied the men crouching by the lead lorry and had picked up Hardman's sten. The noise of gunfire and the stinging whine of bullets ricocheting from the crippled convoy was almost drowned by the whooping shrieks of the Bantu as they appeared and disappeared in the bush, hurling their spears or firing their rifles as they momentarily sprang into view. Mike Delayney uttered a writhing yelp of pain as a bullet smashed his thigh. Morris scrambled desperately towards his mate and was halted in mid-crawl, spinning sideways into the dusty earth and bleeding from two simultaneous hits. Rona Waring huddled white-faced against the front wheel of the lorry, while Holland protected her clumsily with his own body as he fired his sten gun. Jack Foster's mouth opened in a silent gasp of agony as he toppled forwards with a bullet in his back. The hot suffocating air was filled with the scent of sweat and blood, mingled with swirls of smoke and the taste of death.

When the force of the attack had faded and the black warriors had fallen back to re-form for a fresh assault Holland's force of twenty-two men had been cut to less than half.

Holland stopped firing as the shrieks of

their attackers died away. He glanced at the nurse by his side and said huskily:

'Are you all right, Rona?'

She didn't answer. She was staring at Hardman who lay slumped at her feet, her eyes fixed on the pool of red that was slowly spreading across his broad chest. Holland had to repeat his question before his words penetrated into her numbed brain and with an effort she looked up. Her eyes were dulled with shock and her lips quivered uncontrollably. Then she steadied herself and forced herself to speak.

'The — the Sergeant's still alive, Jimmy. I must stop that bleeding.' Her words were horribly cracked and she had to swallow hard before finishing. 'The Red Cross box is in the ambulance.'

'I'll get it for you.'

Holland hardly realised that he was practically begging to be shot as he rose to his feet and stumbled openly to the ambulance. But the Bantu had melted away into the bush and no shot was fired as he reached the cab and pulled open the door. He climbed inside to reach the black metal box with its bright red cross, and the sharp, sudden clang as he accidentally bumped it against the cab door in getting out sounded harshly sacrilegious against the scene of silent carnage. The hush of death had fallen upon the broken convoy, and everywhere sprawled the fallen bodies of their black attackers, their ebony limbs grotesquely twisted and the bright red of their blood soaking swiftly into the arid sand. The wounded lay as silent as the dead, fearful of attracting more murderous gunfire by revealing that they were alive.

Holland staggered slightly as he jumped down from the ambulance, but a firm hand on his arm helped him to regain his balance and then the Red Cross box was taken from him. Holland blinked and then recognised the corporal who had been driving the ambulance. He had not noticed the man crawling out from under the vehicle.

Canning said. 'I'll take that for you, Lieutenant.' And together they hurried back to where Rona Waring was waiting beside Hardman.

The nurse looked up and accepted the first-aid box without speaking. She rested it upon the sand and opened the lid before turning back to the sergeant. She hesitated, swallowed hard, and then began to unbutton his shirt with slow but steady fingers.

Canning looked around the scattered remnants of their escort and his mouth tightened as he counted the bodies of the dead. Of those who were alive a few crouched in readiness for the next attack while their comrades did their best to tend the wounded. Smoke and the burning smell of cordite tainted the air, and the shallow waters of the stream crossing the clearing were veined with mingling swirls of blood from the black corpses lying half submerged.

Grimly Canning turned back to face Holland, his resentment of authority forgotten, and the weight of his two stripes reminding him that even though he was not attached to Holland's command he was still the only capable N.C.O. left.

He said: 'My ambulance is still

undamaged, sir. Would it be best if I put the men who are wounded inside where the nurse can work on them under cover?'

Holland had recovered a little of his composure, and now that the immediate aftermath of silence and realisation of horror had passed he was able to think clearly.

'That's good sense, Corporal, but you'd better hurry.' He winced slightly from the pain of his creased shoulder and then went on. 'They'll be licking their wounds at the moment but it won't be long before their leaders persuade them to attack again. I think we gave them a much hotter fight than they bargained for, but even so they must realise that the next attack will finish us off. They're sure to come back.'

Canning nodded and shouted for Spencer to give him a hand. Spencer came running and then Canning turned towards Holland again.

'I think we'd better get the Sergeant in first. He'll have to go on to one of the beds.'

Rona Waring looked up before Holland could answer. She was pressing a large pad to the bullet hole high on the right side of Hardman's chest and her fingers were already stained with blood.

She said shortly. 'You can't move him yet, Corporal. Not until I get this pad fixed. He shouldn't be moved at all.'

There was again something in the way she framed the word 'Corporal' that flared Canning's resentment for a brief moment. His hostility was not towards her authority, for that would have been too petty in the circumstances. Instead it was a deeper hatred to that intonation that was almost one of contempt, so disdainfully similar to the way Jenny would have spoken. Even at a time like this she had to remind him of the woman he wanted to forget.

Then Holland said 'All right, he'll wait until last. We'll get the remainder of the wounded into the ambulance.'

Swiftly Holland rapped out instructions to the survivors, and while two men watched either side of the trail to detect the first signs of the next attack, the remainder, under the direction of Canning and Spencer, carried the more seriously wounded into the ambulance. The men who had been sheltering behind the last lorry moved up to regroup around Holland, bringing their wounded with them.

The field ambulance carried three beds, two on the right-hand side and one on the left. One of the lower beds was already occupied by the feverish Private Garner, but as he was a lightly built man Canning and Spencer lifted him on to the top bed out of the way. On one of the lower beds they laid Jack Foster, still alive but losing blood fast from the two wounds where a bullet had entered the left-hand side of his back and passed out just below the ribs. Canning did his best to plug the two holes and strap the man up while the rest of the wounded were brought over to the ambulance.

The one remaining bed would be needed for Hardman, but Spencer spread blankets over the floor and there they laid Baxter and Delayney side by side. Delayney was weakly asking for his mate,

Morris, and he swore angrily when the little man was brought inside. Morris was still unconscious, his left arm was smashed and his shrimp-like face was masked with blood from a shallow crease across his temple. The only place they could put him was to prop him in a sitting position at the far end of the ambulance with his knees pushed up against one bed, and his head and shoulders, supported by a pillow, jammed against the other.

Delayney raised himself on one elbow and said through clenched teeth: 'You can't squash him up like that. It ain't bloody right.'

Canning stared at him. 'What the hell else can we do?'

Delayney was sweating in agony from his own bloodied thigh, but ever since he had joined the army he had been demanding the rights of himself and his mates and he was not prepared to stop now.

'I don't know,' he said feebly, 'but it ain't bloody right.'

Canning had no time to argue and

started to leave, but as he did so Delayney
noticed the one bed that had been spared
to take Hardman.

'Here,' he said angrily, 'what's wrong
with that bed.'

'We need it for the Sergeant,' Canning
said. 'He's hurt worse than your mate.'

'You mean that bastard Hardman?'

'That's right. He's been hit in the
chest.'

'I don't give a damn where he's been
hit. My mate needs a bed and he's got
as much right to have one as any bloody
sergeant.'

Canning said grimly: 'It's not a matter
of rights.'

'Well I say it is!' Delayney was
shouting now, his face contorted and
drenched with sweat. 'I say it's bloody
rank distinction, and it's not right.'

Canning almost shouted back. 'For
Christ's sake keep your lawyering for
the barrack room. The Sergeant is more
seriously injured than your mate and
that's all there is to it.'

Delayney started to answer but in the
same moment he inadvertently moved his

smashed thigh and the words were lost in a choking gasp of pain. He fell back on to the blanket-covered floor beside Baxter and without waiting for him to recover Canning left the ambulance and jumped down to the ground.

Spencer was waiting for him, his dark face nervous and no longer smiling and a sten cradled in his arms.

He said: 'Do you think it's going to make any difference, Corp?'

Canning looked at him. 'What's that mean?'

'I mean loading them into the ambulance. The blacks are going to slaughter the lot of us next time they attack. They'll get into the ambulance anyway.'

Canning said flatly: 'Maybe. Maybe not. They lost a lot of men remember — and they're taking a long time in making up their minds to come back. They might have run away altogether.'

Spencer's face failed to register assurance.

Canning said: 'Keep watching the bush, Roy. Stay by the ambulance.' Then he picked up his own sten gun and hurried forward to where Rona Waring was still tending Hardman.

Holland and a pale-faced private were helping to hold the big Sergeant's shoulders off the ground while Rona fixed the last bandage. All three looked up.

Canning said: 'I've managed to squeeze in all the men who are too hurt to fight. There's still one spare bed.'

Holland looked slowly around him. Now that the wounded had been moved away he had only eight men left, most of them bleeding from superficial wounds and cuts. The rest were dead. His transport, except for the already overloaded ambulance, was completely immobilised. His shoulder was throbbing dully and he knew that if the Bantu attacked again his position must be overrun.

He drew a deep breath and then said as calmly as he possibly could: 'Corporal, do you think you can make a break for Kasuvu in the ambulance when the next attack comes? At least we can try and get Nurse Waring and the wounded out of it.'

Canning hesitated, then said: 'I can try it, sir. There is just about enough room for me to pull past this lorry. And once over the stream it's a fairly good road to Kasuvu. If I can once break through them I should be able to keep ahead.'

Rona said suddenly: 'I think that I should stay here with you, Lieutenant. There's a full staff of doctors and nurses at Kasuvu who can take care of the men in the ambulance. I shall be needed here.' The familiar 'Jimmy' had gone now, and she was doing her best to sound formal.

Holland said curtly: 'You'll go in the ambulance. That's an order.'

She straightened her back and said stiffly. 'But there are sure to be more casualties in the next attack. My place is here.'

Holland hesitated. He couldn't bring himself to state the truth; that there would be no casualties at all after the next attack; only the dead. For the next attack must surely bring the end.

At last he repeated 'That's an order,

Lieutenant Waring. You'll go to Kasuvu with the ambulance.'

There was silence as the young officer and the nurse faced each other. Canning crouched a yard away, waiting, and still holding his sten.

Then a new voice said weakly.

'Not Kasuvu, Lieutenant. Not Kasuvu.'

All three looked down at the injured man lying in the dust. It seemed incredible that Hardman with his bullet-smashed chest could possibly be conscious and struggling to speak. But despite the blood he had lost the big Sergeant's eyes were open and his lips were moving feebly. The sweat dripped from every pore of his twisted face, but somewhere deep in the back of his pain-dazed mind was the dominant fact that he was still the Sergeant, and he still owed a duty to the men he had goaded into hating his guts.

He said again: 'Don't try the Kasuvu road, Lieutenant. It's suicide.'

Both Holland and Canning moved closer.

Holland said: 'Why, Sergeant Hardman?

Why should the Kasuvu road be suicide?'

Hardman swallowed weakly, and then rallied his fading strength to continue.

'This whole attack was too well-planned, Lieutenant. A military operation. First they allowed us to get down into the open before they attacked. Second they made sure of destroying our transport. Third they had marked down the radio operator, they killed him and smashed his set.' He broke off, choked huskily, and then forced himself to go on. 'The whole thing was planned to the last detail. The man who planned it knew exactly what he was doing. A man like that would have realised that with only four grenades at his disposal there was a good chance that one of our vehicles might escape destruction. He would have made allowances. He's certain to have built a barrier across the Kasuvu road, somewhere beyond the stream.'

There was a brief, strained silence as Hardman stopped speaking. The big Sergeant had weakened even more with the effort of talking and his head sank back in the dust and his eyes closed.

Holland's face had gone haggard and he turned from Hardman to Canning with defeat in his eyes.

He said: 'The Sergeant's right. The man behind this attack has planned everything too carefully. He must have taken the precaution of blocking the Kasuvu road.'

Canning's face was stubborn and his deep grey eyes were suddenly hard. 'What about Sakinda?' he asked flatly. 'The bush to the left of the track is pretty low, and there's a fifty-fifty chance that I can swing the ambulance completely round without getting bogged down. I can take her back the way we came.'

Hardman's eyes opened again. He made an effort to lift his head but failed. Then the nurse moved to support him.

Hardman said: 'By now the Sakinda road may be blocked too — they've had time to move in behind us.'

He became silent again, but this time his eyes remained open.

Canning said nothing. It was Holland's decision.

Holland's lips were bloodless and the

torment of responsibility was mirrored in his eyes. He looked desperately at Hardman but the big Sergeant had sunk back into the depths of pain. Hardman's job was to use his experience to assess the facts and then to advise, and now his part was finished. It was up to the Lieutenant to give the orders.

Holland said at last: 'Get the Sergeant into the ambulance, Corporal. The moment the next attack starts you will make an attempt to get back to Sakinda. There is a possibility that the road may be blocked by now, but that's a chance you'll have to take.' He faltered, and then ended harshly: 'Here, there is no chance at all.'

Canning said quietly: 'I'll do my best, sir.' He glanced at the man who had been helping to support Hardman. 'Give me a hand to carry the Sergeant. I'll take his shoulders.'

The private was pale-faced beneath a coating of dust and sweat, but something, perhaps discipline, perhaps the presence of the nurse, kept him under control. He lifted the big Sergeant's legs while

Canning hooked both arms under the man's armpits, and, both staggering slightly, they carried him across to the ambulance.

Mike Delayney was conscious again as they lifted Hardman on to the bed, and something that might have been satisfaction mingled with the pain lines on his twisted face. He said vindictively: 'At least one of those black bastards deserves a medal.' But he lacked the strength to argue any more about Morris having the bed.

Holland had stayed back, and for a moment he and Rona Waring were alone. Her face was white and strained and her light blue eyes had a glazed look. She had lost her cap and there was dust and sand in her blonde hair. She was sweating almost as much as the men. Somewhat clumsily Holland offered her a handkerchief to wipe Hardman's blood from her fingers.

He said quietly, 'Get in the ambulance, Rona. The next attack could start at any moment.' His voice faltered again before he finished. 'The Corporal looks pretty

59

competent. I think he'll get you back to Sakinda.'

There was a lot Rona Waring wanted to say. She didn't want to go with the surly-faced Corporal, and she hated to leave Holland. She looked into his haggard yet still boyish face, and she badly wanted to attend to his injured shoulder. But she knew that he still wouldn't allow it, not while there were more seriously wounded men in the ambulance. Her mouth was dry and she couldn't say anything, not even good-bye.

Holland rested his hand on her arm and squeezed reassuringly, forcing himself to smile. Then he led her over to the ambulance.

Canning and Spencer waited by the open doors.

Holland said, 'Don't get into the cab until I give the signal for you to make a break. There's no doubt that they've been watching every move we've made, but if you men take up your positions underneath the ambulance again until the actual attack starts, we might fool them into thinking that you're staying to fight it out. We'll give you covering fire as you get into the cab, and if you can break through them as they're closing in it will give them less time to realise what's happening.'

Canning said, 'We can do it, sir.'

'I hope so.' Holland lacked the Corporal's self assurance. He went on, 'When you reach Sakinda you'll be able to join up with Sergeant Riley. Get him to escort you to safer territory by another route. He's got another radio operator with him so he can call up reinforcements if necessary.'

Canning saluted. He turned to the nurse and said, 'You'd better get inside, Lieutenant. I'll close the doors behind you.'

He moved to help her climb aboard, and then he saw that Delayney was fully conscious again and watching him.

Delayney said, 'We going back to Sakinda, Corp?'

'That's right.'

A light gleamed in Delayney's eyes. 'Then get me my sten, Corp. And leave the doors open. Some of them niggers are sure to chase us, and I can sort them out a bit.'

Canning looked down at him. Delayney lay on his back with the blood from his smashed thigh soaking into the blanket on the floor beneath him.

Rona Waring said abruptly, 'He isn't fit. You can't expect him to fire a sten.'

Canning said slowly, 'We can turn him over on his stomach. And we do need someone to hold off any pursuit. Spencer and I can only effectively cover the road ahead and the sides.'

Delayney grinned weakly and added, 'Besides, the bastards shot my mate. They ain't getting away with that.'

Holland hesitated, then he turned to the private who had helped to carry Hardman across and said wearily:

'Do as the man says. Give him his sten.'

There was a movement from Baxter, lying on the floor beside Delayney. His eyes were closed but he had been conscious all the while, suffering in silence from the pain of his broken foot and ankle. Now he opened his eyes and said simply:

'Make that two sten guns. I can fire one as well.'

As gently as possible Canning and Spencer turned the two men over on to their stomachs so that they could face the open doors. Delayney almost fainted again in the process and both he and Baxter had turned a deathly whitish-grey when the job was completed. Rona Waring packed pillows around Delayney's thigh and beneath Baxter's foot to make them as comfortable as possible. She had a small amount of morphia, and although she had already given a shot to Hardman there was still enough left to give them both a pain-killing injection. The two sten guns were handed into the ambulance and Delayney accepted his with a crooked smile.

Holland said, 'Good luck, men.' His eyes met Rona's for a moment and he felt a cold fist squeezing at his heart. With the men listening there was nothing that he could say.

She held his gaze helplessly, and then managed to say:

'Good luck, Lieutenant.'

He said 'thank you,' and thought that the words were going to get stuck in his throat. It seemed impossible that there was nothing else to be said in that moment.

He turned away reluctantly. Canning was beside him.

Holland said, 'You'd better crawl back beneath the ambulance, Corporal. I'll give a shout when the moment comes to make a break.' He tried to smile. 'Good luck.'

Canning raised his hand in a final salute. He couldn't bring himself to say good luck. It was so pointless and made everything seem unreal, like a scene from a comic strip or a boy's adventure annual.

Holland returned the salute and then hurried to join his men who were keeping low around the wreckage of the lead lorry.

Canning called to Spencer and they swiftly wriggled back beneath the ambulance, each man again covering opposite sides of the track.

Canning's mouth was dry now as he waited with his sten nestling against his shoulder. It was only ten or fifteen minutes since the last attack had stopped and he wondered how much longer it would be before the Bantu came screaming at them again. He stared into the bush with aching eyes but the only black bodies he saw were those of the dead. He wondered whether thc delay meant that the tribesmen were making absolutely sure of killing them all by blocking off the one route of retreat to Sakinda before launching the last assault.

If that was so he would be driving the ambulance straight into a trap, and he would not have the ghost of a chance of turning twice to rejoin Holland once he had broken away.

For the first time he felt fear padding softly along the length of his spine.

Death Without Glory

The heat was murderous and there was complete silence about the clearing where the wrecked convoy lay halted before the stream. No wind stirred the dry, scrub branches of the bush, or the deeper tangles of thickening jungle. The ever-flitting birds and the hordes of chattering monkeys had fled into the more distant branches of the forest at the first signs of battle, and now there were no signs of life whatsoever.

Canning began to wonder hopefully whether the Bantu might have fled also; whether they might have lost heart at their first heavy losses and be even now running away along hidden forest paths. Was it possible that they were afraid to attack a third time, even though their overwhelming numbers must bring them success?

Canning watched and waited, and slowly the hope died. It was too quiet.

If the Bantu had gone then the birds and the monkeys would have raised the courage to return. The black warriors must still be there, silent and unseen in the bush.

What were they waiting for?

Canning could taste dust in his mouth, and became suddenly conscious of the fact that he was terribly thirsty. He passed his tongue over his lips and tasted the salt of his own sweat where it ran in a slow trickle down the side of his nose. Christ, he thought, why can't they attack and get it over. He began to wonder whether he really would have the guts to crawl out from under the ambulance and make the near suicide dash for his cab once the attack actually started. It had been easy enough to assure the Lieutenant that he could do it, but now that he had time to think about it he wasn't sure. Fear could very easily pin him down to the dirt beneath his vehicle.

Why didn't they attack? What the hell were they waiting for.

He stared into the dusty bush and

told himself that they must be there. The birds and the monkeys were still silent so they must be there.

He glanced sideways at Spencer, but all he could see was his friend's boots, the once polished toes digging into the dirt. He knew that Spencer was even more scared than he was and a new thought filled him with sudden horror: suppose he got to the cab and found that Roy had been afraid to move; would he have to drive forwards over his own mate? Could he make a decision like that?

Savagely he pushed the thought down. Roy wouldn't be petrified. He wasn't that scared. Why the hell didn't those damned blacks attack? He wasn't as jittery as this when there was something to do, some fighting to be done. Blast the heat and the dust. Why the hell did he have to be here anyhow. He didn't care a damn what happened to the bloody Congo.

For Christ sake why don't they attack!

His hand was trembling slightly on the trigger of the sten. He pulled it away and carefully wiped the sweat from his eyes, controlling his tumbling thoughts with an effort. And then he saw a slight swaying movement from a low thorny bush barely five yards from the edge of the road.

His hand slapped down on the sten again and he fired. The sound roared in the still air and the thorn-bush threshed wildly under the impact. A rising scream echoed above the snarl of the sten, gurgling in mid-note as black limbs fluttered in agony.

Screams and gunfire burst like a clap of thunder and immediately the bush was alive with yelling black warriors, rising to their feet and charging savagely. They had been silently and painstakingly inching their way through the low scrub until now they were almost on top of the crippled convoy.

Canning stopped thinking and became part of the living sten gun that reverberated ferociously against his shoulder. Nothing existed except the flashes of flame spurting from the gun muzzle and the black, negroid faces contorting in the grip of death and falling away before that withering fire. Spencer was firing with equally killing effect as a second wave of the Bantu hurled themselves at the opposite flank, and from Holland's position by the lead lorry more sten guns chattered in savage defiance. Three of Holland's men fell in the unmistakable finality of death and two more reeled back wounded before the oncoming tide was halted.

Canning fired the last rounds in his magazine and then deftly slammed a fresh magazine into place. For a moment there was a lull in the firing as the Bantu momentarily gave ground. And then Holland bawled frantically.

'Now, Corporal. NOW!'

Canning didn't hesitate. He shouted to Spencer to follow him and scrambled swiftly into the open. There were yells from the Bantu and he swung his sten in a raking half-circle that kept them at bay as he sprinted for his cab. A broad-bladed spear scored through the red paint that marked the big cross on the side of the ambulance and bounced away again with a savage clang. Several of the shiny rifles cracked in eager black hands and the bullets whined off the metal work beside Canning's head as he yanked open the cab door. Holland and two of his men covered him as best they could as he pulled himself behind the wheel. He got the door shut and ducked beneath it just in time to shut out another shower of spears and arrows. A bullet shattered the glass of the windscreen.

Canning raised himself up, thrust the snout of the sten through the open window and fired another burst. Then he ducked down again and started the engine. Mercifully it coughed into life at the first attempt.

He looked round desperately for Spencer. The noise of gunfire and screaming was deafening and he felt a moment of panic. Where was Spencer? Could he still be underneath the ambulance, or had he been killed before he could reach the cab. Canning suddenly realised that he hadn't a hope in hell without his co-driver beside him. He couldn't fire his sten and drive at the same time and he needed Spencer to cover him.

Then there was a scrambling noise at

71

the far side door and he leaned across the cab to thrust it open. He saw Spencer's face, dark and frightened. The men around Holland were still providing covering fire as Canning hauled his companion bodily into the ambulance.

Spencer still held his sten and he used the muzzle to smash away the fragments of broken glass that still clung to the frame of the windscreen. He shouted hysterically:

'Get her moving, Corp. For Christ's sake get her moving.'

Canning rammed the ambulance into gear and brought his foot off the clutch simultaneously. He pulled frantically at the wheel to bring the heavy vehicle lurching out of line and there was a grating crash as the off-side wing scraped against the back end of the lorry in front. Then the ambulance was swinging out in a half-circle and Canning put his foot hard down as they crashed through the low scrub bushes off the side of the road. Spencer cleared the way ahead of them with another burst from his sten. A terrified black face disappeared beneath the high bonnet and the ambulance jolted crazily as the wheels ground the man's body into the dust. Just clear of the ambulance's path a sweating young warrior aimed his brand new rifle carefully at Canning's head, an expression of savage delight on his crudely tattooed face. Then a short burst from Spencer's sten crucified him against a thorn-bush before he could pull the rifle's trigger. Canning kept his head down and strained at the wheel to bring the ambulance round. For a moment the rear wheels skidded and churned in the dust, and then they gripped again and the ambulance lurched on. Seconds later they completed the circle and jolted back on to the Sakinda road.

Canning straightened the wheel and then crashed the ambulance into second gear. Spears and bullets skidded off the vehicle's sides in a rattling nightmare of sound. Canning thrust his foot flat to the floor and huddled as close to the wheel as possible as he aimed the ambulance back the way they had come. There was a slight bend in the road and he felt panic again with the sudden blinding certainty that the road would be blocked beyond. Then they were tearing through clutching branches as he took the bend and relief gave him new strength as he saw that there was a clear road, there was no barrier.

The ambulance had crashed through the cordon of attacking tribesmen, and now there were shrieks of rage as the Bantu swarmed in pursuit. They filled the road in a solid, running mass, frantically hurling their spears and shooting with both bows and arrows and rifles. They had almost caught up with the lumbering ambulance when abruptly the doors flew wide open. Delayney and Baxter opened fire with their stens in the same moment.

The Bantu were so closely packed that it was impossible to miss. The front rank came tumbling to their knees and the pursuit became chaos. Delayney was grinning insanely as he blazed away with his sten gun and he thought suddenly that it didn't even matter if he killed the black who deserved the medal. This was vengeance for his mate Morris and his own shattered thigh. Baxter was grimly purposeful, his lean face completely devoid of feeling as he squinted along the barrel of his sten.

The ambulance suddenly bucked wildly as the front wheel hit a massive tree root that sprawled out into the road. Delayney's body arched with agony as the vibration tore through his wounded thigh, his fingers opened spasmodically and the sten gun slipped over the back of the ambulance and was left behind on the dirt road as unconsciousness swept over him.

Baxter stiffened in agony with the jolting, but he didn't faint and kept on firing.

Rona Waring crouched helplessly in the back of the ambulance, staring in horror at the carnage they were leaving behind.

★ ★ ★

Holland and the pitiful handful of men who remained beside him had received a brief respite as most of the attacking warriors on their left flank ran in chase of the ambulance. But it was only temporary. Within minutes the near-naked champions of Katanga were turning back, more angry and murderous than before. A straight stretch of road had enabled Canning to get into top gear and pull clear away, and the raging Bantu had swiftly returned to the more easy prey.

Holland had five men left, and two of those were wounded. They lay flat, half underneath the wrecked lorry and firing steadily. Holland felt his stomach squirm at the smell of blood and the sight of smashed bodies, both black and white, around him. The sten gun was hot in his hands and he began to pray that the first bullet to hit him would kill him outright. The sweating face of a private beside him was suddenly wiped out by a red mushroom of blood as a bullet hit the man just below the nose.

The Bantu had closed the cordon again and several of them had taken cover behind the twisted metal of the second lorry. Many more were screaming and yelling from the bush. Then there was another concerted rush.

Holland thought, this is it, and closed his eyes. It was suddenly futile to kill any more and his hands relaxed around his sten. He waited for death.

Instead there was a sudden commanding shout, and then incredibly the firing and the screaming stopped and there was unbelievable silence.

Holland opened his eyes and saw a white man coming slowly through the ring of hesitant tribesmen. He shouted another order in the Bantu tongue and Holland felt a swirl of hope. The man was tall and darkly bronzed, and he carried a rifle in his hand. He was obviously the mercenary who had been directing the battle, and was probably the man Holland had been sent to find, but at least he was white.

Holland stared at him, noting the faded bush shirt and tropical shorts, the bare, muscular arms and thighs and the tense lines around the hard mouth. He looked like a man with no conscience, but at least he was white. No white man would let them be butchered now that the battle was over.

Then a slim young negro, naked but for a flapping loin cloth, leaped defiantly to his feet, and deliberately hurled his spear. Holland ducked instinctively as the broad blade sliced over his head and realised with terrible despair that the mercenary had no real control over his black soldiers.

For the second time Holland accepted the imminence of death, but then a new voice repeated the mercenary's order. A thin but impressive old man pushed his way to the front. He was naked but for a dirty grey loin cloth and his cheeks were heavily tatooed, but he also carried a brand new rifle that gave him added stature. This was Mambiro, chief of the Bantu. He signed to the mercenary to go ahead.

The tall man moved forwards and said curtly:

'Order your men to throw down their guns, Lieutenant. The fighting is over.'

Holland looked round. He had two fit men, and two wounded. The rest were dead. He nodded his head wearily and laid down his own sten gun. The others followed his example. With an effort Holland stood up.

'Who are you?' he asked.

The mercenary shrugged. 'My name is Larocque — if that is important.'

'I suppose it was you who planned this.'

Larocque nodded. 'I planned it. I fired the first signal shot which should have killed you. I fired the shots that smashed your radio transmitter. And it was I who picked off your Sergeant.' He was searching the faces of the remaining four soldiers as he spoke, and suddenly he turned angrily to Mambiro. He said harshly, 'The man whose picture I showed you — he isn't here!'

The old negro shrugged. It was unimportant now.

Larocque cursed and strode swiftly over to the lorry. He glared down at the faces of the dead soldiers and turned one man over who lay on his stomach. Holland watched him helplessly, sudden fury replacing the nausea in his bowels.

Larocque walked over to the last lorry and carefully examined the faces of the dead men who lay there. He walked forward again to stare closely at the blood-smeared features of the jeep driver who still lay crushed beneath his vehicle. Then he came back to Holland. His face was thunderous and his knuckles showed white where he gripped his rifle. He dug into the pocket of his bush shirt with the fingers of his left hand and took out the photograph he had passed around the Bantu warriors before the attack. He showed it to Holland.

'Recognise him, Lieutenant? He was one of your men wasn't he?'

Holland recognised the man in the photograph, but he shook his head slowly.

'Why do you want him?'

'That's my business.' Larocque suddenly looked down the line of wrecked vehicles and realisation dawned in his eyes. 'The ambulance!' he said sharply, 'It's gone. I thought I heard the sound of an engine roaring during that last battle.' He pivoted on his heel to face Mambiro and uttered a single sentence in Bantu.

Mambiro shrugged, and inclined his head.

Larocque cursed. 'The bloody fools. They let him get away.' He jerked back to Holland. 'He was aboard that ambulance, wasn't he? He must have been.'

Holland said nothing.

Larocque pushed the crumpled photograph back into his pocket.

'They've gone back to Sakinda,' he grated, 'They must have done. I blocked the road on the other side of the stream.'

Holland felt suddenly grateful to Hardman. If the big Sergeant had not stopped him he would have sent the ambulance with its load of wounded men straight into the road block. Then he realised that the ambulance was still in danger and lied calmly.

'The man in that photograph was not one of my men. I did get several of the wounded away in the ambulance, but none of them resembles the man you are looking for.'

Larocque gave him a hard stare. 'You're lying, Lieutenant. I saw him here just before I fired that first shot. I'm sure I saw him.'

There was an element of doubt in the last sentence and Holland played on it desperately.

'You were wrong. With every man here wearing khaki it's easy to make a mistake.'

Larocque said slowly, 'There's only one way to find out, and that's to catch up with your ambulance and look for myself.'

Holland realised with a sinking heart that nothing he said would make any difference. The two men faced each other and then Mambiro came closer with short, waddling steps.

The old negro pursed his thick lips and said impatiently:

'Talk finished? Enough talk!'

Larocque stepped back. He said to Holland:

'As the old boy says, talk is useless.'

Mambiro turned and raised a hand to his warriors.

Holland saw what was coming. He shouted desperately:

82

'Larocque, you're a white man. You can't let them butcher us!'

Larocque hesitated, looking at Mambiro. The negro said harshly:

'They are our enemies. The enemies of Katanga!'

The Belgian mercenary looked apologetically at Holland. 'I'm sorry, Lieutenant,' he said slowly. And then he walked away. The ranks of the waiting Bantu opened to let him through, and then Mambiro stepped aside and waved his hand.

The black warriors uttered shrieking yells of triumph, and disregarding their rifles they rushed in with knives and spears. It was all over in a very few minutes.

Flight Into the Bush

Canning drove as fast as he dared along the rutted Sakinda road. The fine dust had blown into his mouth and eyes and he was half-blind as he struggled to control the wildly swaying ambulance. Large particles of sand grated between his clenched teeth with a sharp wincing sound and caused his head to shudder uncontrollably. The backs of his fists were pure white where the knuckle bones thrust hard against the skin, and the tendons had stiffened into a network of knotted vines along his arms. His palms were wet with sweat and with every lurch of the ambulance the steering wheel threatened to tear free from his slippery fingers. He had left the scene of the ambush far behind now, but he gave no thought to slackening speed.

Spencer sat rigidly beside him, one hand clinging to the cab door for support and the other still clamped around his sten.

In the back of the ambulance Rona Waring was standing upright and hanging on to the upper bed for support. The open doors were swinging and rattling crazily on their hinges and through them she watched the dust-shrouded track falling away in their wake. The road was flanked by vicious wait-a-bit thorns and waist high yellow grass, and tall, spiky acacias and dense thickets of thorn-bush rose above the surrounding savannah plain.

Baxter was the only one of the wounded men who still remained conscious. He lay with his face pressed hard against the floor and his teeth locked together as he fought off the spasms of pain that flooded upwards from the toes of his left foot with every jolt. He had pulled his sten gun well back into the ambulance and now it lay unheeded on the blanket beside him.

Rona's eyes were dull as she stared down the trail they were leaving behind. They had covered a good two or three miles since the Bantu had given up the chase, but she could still see a vivid mental picture of the howling warriors charging towards her; their shrieks still echoed in her mind and the pure butchery as Delayney and Baxter had opened fire into the packed bodies had stunned her into a state of blank shock.

Then the ambulance crashed through another pothole and this time Baxter was unable to suppress the retching gasp of agony that was torn from his throat. Rona heard the sound and slowly became alive to the immediate scene around her.

Both Hardman and Foster were in critical condition and there was fresh blood seeping through the thick padding of bandages around Hardman's chest. Morris had been shaken from his hunched position at the back of the ambulance and his limp body had toppled over to press heavily against her knees. His arm had started to bleed again and he looked smaller than ever as he lay crumpled at her feet.

Until now she had not been conscious of Morris's weight pinning her against the beds and when she tried to move she almost fell on top of him. The ambulance swayed again and she grabbed at the top bed to stop herself going down. Through the open communication panel she could see the back of Canning's head as he hunched over the wheel and she was suddenly and unreasonably furious at his reckless driving.

'Stop it!' she screamed. 'Stop it you bloody fool! You'll kill them all!'

Canning heard her but it took a few seconds for the words to penetrate. Then reluctantly he began to slacken speed.

Rona steadied herself and then said curtly, 'Slow down, Corporal. Slow down and stop.'

Canning looked back at her. His grey eyes were red-rimmed from the smarting effect of the dust and his lips were compressed into a tight line. He had lost his beret and his dark hair, normally swept back, had fallen down the side of his face to be plastered against his skin by a mixture of sweat and dust.

He said, 'We haven't got time to stop. Can't you patch them up while we're moving?'

'How the hell can I do anything with you bouncing the ambulance all over the road. These men are all badly wounded, they can't take that kind of hammering until I can get them properly strapped up.'

Canning said harshly. 'The road to Sakinda follows a wide curve to circle round thick bush and forest. But the Bantu don't have to follow the road, they can cut through the jungle paths to head us off. And if they do get ahead then all the bandages in the world won't help any of us.'

Rona felt her anger flaring again.

'Corporal, you'll stop this ambulance. That's an order.'

Canning's expression masked his feelings as he turned his head away from her and slowly braked the heavy ambulance to a stop. Then he turned to Spencer, still sitting in rigid silence beside him:

'Roy, take your sten and get up on the roof. Keep a watch all the way round while I give the Lieutenant a hand.' He deliberately tried to make the word Lieutenant sound as insulting as her pronunciation of Corporal.

Spencer hesitated, then he moistened

his dry lips and said huskily, 'Right, Corp.'

He pushed open the cab door and Canning watched him pull himself on to the roof.

Tightening his mouth again Canning got down from the cab and walked to the back of the ambulance. His feet kicked fresh dust clouds from the road and the sun enveloped him in an invisible blanket of heat. He pulled himself into the back of the ambulance, stepping carefully to avoid Baxter and Delayney who occupied most of the floor space.

For a moment he appraised the situation, and almost immediately he had to concede that the nurse had been right. Hardman and Foster both looked more dead than alive, and if he had continued to drive at the same furious pace he would undoubtedly have killed them. He looked up into her face and said briefly:

'We'd better get on with it.'

He placed his feet gingerly as he stepped over Delayney to move Morris's unconscious body away from her legs. He lifted the little man easily and propped him back in his original hunched position at the back of the ambulance.

Rona straightened up and reached for her medical box.

'We'll look after the private on the bottom bed first, Corporal. I think he's the worst.'

Foster was in a serious condition. His face was the colour of dirty linen and his breathing was very ragged and shallow. Canning supported him while Rona rearranged the top layer of his bandages to strap the wounds up more tightly. It was obvious that he needed hospital attention if he was going to live.

When they had done all they could for him they moved on to Hardman. Technically the big Sergeant was more critically wounded than Foster, but his bull-like constitution was supporting him well. Hardman could not have been more aptly named. Again there was nothing much that Rona could do for him except tighten his bandages to stop the bleeding.

They turned Delayney on to his back

to make him more comfortable and then cut away his trouser leg to clear his right thigh. The bullet had entered from the front, smashed the bone and then sheered away through the soft muscle at the back. Rona cleaned the wound as best she could and strapped it up, thankful that the man was unconscious as she did so.

Baxter was not so lucky. Despite his tall, rangy figure he had a constitution that almost matched Hardman's, and he had defiantly refused to allow unconsciousness to swamp over him. Now he gritted his teeth while his injured foot and ankle received further attention. When Canning suggested turning him over he shook his head, preferring to remain as he was.

When they turned to Morris the little man had recovered and was watching them with pain-blurred eyes. He looked down at Delayney and then up at the nurse.

'Is Irish going to be all right, Miss?' he asked anxiously.

Rona managed to give him a faint smile.

'He'll be all right,' she said. 'They'll take good care of him when we get you all to hospital.' She had to make an effort to keep her voice from breaking because she knew that Delayney would never properly walk again. To cover up she turned to Canning and said coldly, 'We've run out of bandages, Corporal. Tear up one of the sheets and make some more.'

For a few moments Canning had felt the beginning of a grudging sense of respect for the unflinching determination with which the nurse had tended her patients with such limited resources, but her tone put the barrier between them again. Without answering he took a sheet from Foster's bed and began angrily ripping it into strips.

Rona had turned to Morris:

'This may hurt,' she said quietly. 'But I've got to clean your arm up a bit before I bandage it, and I've nothing left to kill the pain.'

Morris forced a pale grin on to his shrivelled face.

'Don't mind me, Miss,' he said. 'I'm

a coward. I shall probably faint.'

Rona found another smile. 'That's the most sensible thing to do.'

Canning handed her some strips of the torn sheet and she began to clean off the blood on the little man's arm. A bullet had chipped the bone and passed clean through the muscle. Morris winced and breathed harshly through his teeth as she worked, but he didn't faint. When she had bandaged his arm she cleaned the worst of the blood off his face and bound up the glancing wound across his temple. At last she sat back and Morris opened his eyes.

'Thanks, Miss,' he said weakly.

Rona smiled an acknowledgement and then stood upright. She turned to face Canning who waited beside her.

'You'd better drive on now, Corporal. But drive slowly and cause as little jolting as possible. Hardman and Foster have already lost too much blood, and I don't want their wounds re-opened again.'

Canning knew that she was right, speed would cost them at least two lives and they would have to take a chance on the Bantu being able to head them off. He began to hope that Holland and his men were still holding out and keeping the tribesmen occupied, or failing that, that the Bantu would be satisfied with their victory at the stream and would not attempt to pursue the ambulance any farther.

Rona went on: 'It shouldn't take too many hours to get back to Sakinda, even with driving carefully. Once there I'll get Sergeant Riley to radio for a helicopter to fly these men out.'

Canning said briefly, 'Yes, Ma'am.'

He stepped back over Delayney and Baxter and jumped down on to the road. He closed the big double doors and then called up to Spencer. Almost immediately Spencer appeared on the edge of the roof looking down.

'We're moving on again,' Canning told him. 'There's nothing else we can do for the wounded until we can get them back to Sakinda.'

Spencer looked as though the strain of waiting had frayed at his nerves. He said shakily, 'All right, Corp. I'm coming down.'

He moved forward to climb down the side of the cab and Canning helped him drop the last few feet. Spencer still held his sten as though it were glued to his fingers, and his shoulders trembled slightly as Canning touched him.

Canning realised that Spencer needed something to think about, something to take his mind off the possibility of a fresh attack. He said firmly:

'You'd better drive, Roy. Take it as slowly and smoothly as you can. We don't want to shake the lads up in the back any more than we have to.'

Spencer nodded and climbed into the driving seat without argument. Canning circled the ambulance's bonnet and swung into the opposite side of the cab. Spencer hesitated, and then very reluctantly he relaxed his grip on his sten gun and laid it down beside him. He started the ambulance and rolled her forwards, settling himself grimly into the driving position.

Canning felt easier. Driving would not

take Spencer's mind wholly away from the thoughts that disturbed him, but at least it would help. Besides, he was beginning to realise that his own arms and shoulders ached from the enforced tension of driving out of the ambush at the stream, and he was glad to rest and let his co-driver take over.

The road was the same endless, roofless tunnel through dense thorn thickets and tangles of sun-yellowed scrub. It was now almost noon and the sun was directly overhead, a fiercely blazing sword of Damocles suspended in the vast blue emptiness of the sky. The ambulance followed its own wheel tracks back towards Sakinda and Canning tried to relax.

In the back Rona Waring sat on the edge of Hardman's bed and tried to steady the over-fast beating of her heart. After the first daze of shock had worn off there had been the task of tending the injured men to fill her mind, but now that there was nothing else that she could do her thoughts had brought fear crowding back into her heart again. She knew that by now Holland and his men must surely be dead or prisoners, and she prayed that the young Lieutenant might still be alive, even if only as a captive of the Bantu. She knew too that Canning had good grounds to fear that the Bantu might head them off before they reached Sakinda and she was terribly afraid. If the black tribesmen caught up with the ambulance then Canning and the men would only have death to face, but she was a woman, and she could not rid her mind of the vile things that they might do to her before she was allowed to die.

She was almost glad when Jack Foster began to moan weakly in a delirium and she had to move across the ambulance to hold him still. By moving he could open up his wounds again and she pinned him down by the shoulders and spoke softly to quieten him down. She barely knew what she was saying, but it didn't really matter. The man needed her help and that in itself was enough to put a brake on her thoughts.

Foster's movements ceased, for he was too weak to offer any resistance to her weight. She relaxed and then there was a fresh creaking from the bed above her and she heard Garner begin to stir and moan. In all the confusion of the past few hours she had completely forgotten her original patient.

Wearily she straightened up. Garner's eyes were closed and he was still unconscious, but he was beginning to twist fretfully on his bed. She tried to hold him still and then Foster began to move again.

Rona hesitated, not knowing which man to help first. Then she remembered that there were two men in the cab and called sharply:

'Corporal! Will one of you men come back here and help me please. It only needs one of you to drive.'

Canning's hand had automatically reached for his sten gun as she shouted, and he felt suddenly guilty as he realised that even his nerves were balanced on edge. He turned to Spencer and said:

'I'll go, Roy. You can carry on driving.'

Spencer nodded and slowed the ambulance to a halt. Canning dropped down on to the road still holding his sten and slammed the cab door behind him. He walked round to the back and hesitated before opening the doors, suddenly wondering why he had taken it upon himself to help the nurse instead of sending Spencer. Then he decided sourly that it was too late to change his mind, and pulling open the doors he climbed into the back of the ambulance. He shut the doors behind him and shouted to Spencer to drive on.

Rona said quietly, 'Look after Private Garner, Corporal. He's twisting about in his sleep. I can't hold two men down at the same time.'

Canning laid his sten on the floor. 'Yes, Ma'am,' he said flatly. And then he stepped over Delayney's body to examine Garner.

Rona sat at the head of the lower bunk and concentrated on keeping Foster still. She had seen the sullen look that came into Canning's eyes when she had adressed him, and she too wished that he had sent Spencer back instead. At least the dark youth was civil.

Canning was strongly aware of her sitting only inches away from him as he wiped the sweat from Garner's temples with a piece of torn sheet, and the very nearness of her reminded him again of Jenny. It was ironic to think that he had welcomed this posting to the Congo because he had hoped that it would help him to forget his ex-fiancée, only to find that he was expected to work with her double. He didn't even have to think of Jenny to remember what she looked like, he had only to glance at Rona Waring with her fair hair and baby blue eyes and the memory was complete. Even the haughty sound of her voice was almost identical to Jenny's.

For a moment he forgot the ambulance and the sick man stirring slightly beneath his restraining hands, and his thoughts flitted back through time. Back to England and an unusually hot October afternoon. Jenny was not expecting him, but he had unexpectedly found himself in the region of her Kensington flat and he knew that she should be at home.

He didn't bother to knock, simply

letting himself in with the key she had given him. They were due to be married in five months and he knew the flat better than he knew his own home. The small living-room was empty and he felt a sense of disappointment. He recalled that she had had a modelling engagement for that morning and supposed that it must have delayed her longer than she had anticipated. For a moment he hesitated, not sure whether he ought to leave and come back later. Then he decided that she would probably turn up at any moment, and that in the meantime he would make himself a cup of coffee and wait.

He crossed to the small kitchenette and saw with satisfaction that there was still coffee in the percolator. It only needed heating. He began to whistle tunelessly to himself. The noise brought a sudden movement from the bedroom and he stopped whistling and smiled. She was home after all, probably just changing into something relaxing.

Then the bedroom door opened and Canning's smile slowly died as he stared at the man who came out.

The man was big and paunchy with grey hair and a florid face. He wore no jacket but his cream shirt looked expensive and big gold links glinted at the cuffs. His dark grey trousers were clearly part of an equally expensive suit. To Canning he was a total stranger.

He said sharply, 'What the hell are you doing here?'

There was a movement behind him, and Canning saw Jenny in the bedroom doorway. She wore a filmy *négligé* that reached to her knees and nothing else. Canning knew that there would be nothing else beneath it. Her hand flickered to her throat and stayed there, her eyes widening in fear. She started to move back into the bedroom and then hesitated, as if realising that it was already too late.

The stranger said again, 'Who the hell are you?'

Canning looked past him. He said harshly:

'Who is he, Jenny?'

She swallowed hard, her white throat

working convulsively before she could answer.

'David, you — you don't understand. This is Mr. Harvey. He runs a modelling agency. He — he arranges all my jobs.'

Harvey turned on her savagely. 'What the hell — '

Canning said, 'Shut up, Mister.' And each word had the steely ring of controlled fury.

Harvey was the bigger man, but for the moment he held his tongue.

Canning stared with disgust at the girl he had intended to marry. He couldn't say anything and his muscles were knotted with the burning desire to smash into the pair of them. He had to keep his fists close at his sides and his face was dark with fury.

Jenny said desperately, 'David, you don't understand. You're a nice boy, and I did want to marry you. But — '

Canning said harshly, 'The engagement ring I gave you cost me twenty-five pounds. Where is it?'

Her voice lost its faltering note and she said sullenly:

'I haven't got it.'

Canning barely noticed the change in her tone.

'Where is it?'

The baby blue eyes became suddenly brazen and the change was complete. She had recognised the end and all pretence was gone.

She said flatly, 'I pawned it. I haven't had a modelling job in six weeks so I pawned it. You can have the ticket if you like.'

Canning's control snapped. He lunged forward and coiled one fist around the neckline of the *négligé*. He dragged her past Harvey and the flimsy material ripped. She flung up her arms to protect her face and staggered back naked as the torn nylon came fully away in Canning's hand. Harvey pushed his big bulk clumsily between them.

'Now wait a minute, Soldier boy. You can't — '

Canning drove his fist with savage force into the man's paunchy belly and Harvey's expression became contorted by agony and surprise. He looked as though the last thing he had expected was for Canning to get violent about the affair.

Canning hit him again and the big man sagged to his knees. Despite his size Harvey was soft and there wasn't an ounce of fight in him. Canning hooked his fist full into the florid face and Harvey choked and gagged as he toppled over to the floor.

Jenny turned to run into the bedroom but Canning caught her in three strides. He grabbed her wrist and she screamed as he spun her round. She writhed in his grip but the squirming nakedness that would have once excited him now repulsed him and he slapped the back of his hand hard across her face.

She landed on the bed with tears in her eyes, and slowly Canning felt the anger drain out of him. He had loved her once, and he suddenly found that even now he could not hit her again.

He realised slowly that there was nothing left to say, and nothing left to do. Jenny flinched away from him when he moved but he simply turned away and walked out. Harvey looked up at him as he passed, wiping the blood from his mouth and staring with bewildered eyes.

Canning felt almost sorry for Harvey. The man had taken a beating for a tramp who wasn't even worth it. He left the flat and walked through Kensington to the nearest pub, and there he got blind, stinking drunk for the first time in his life. Three weeks later his battalion had been flown out to the Congo, and he had been glad to leave England behind.

The ambulance jolted through an unavoidable pot-hole and the movement slowly pulled Canning out of the past. There was fresh sweat on Garner's forehead and he wiped it away with careful fingers. He glanced around the ambulance and saw that only Baxter and Morris were awake. Baxter silent and unmoving on the floor, Morris miserably caressing his injured arm.

Rona Waring sat with her head bowed over Foster, her hands still pressing down on his shoulders. Canning stared down at the top of her fair head and felt the bitter hurt stirring again in his chest. Why the hell did she have to look so much like Jenny?

The ambulance moved steadily on and they had covered almost half the distance back to Sakinda now. Spencer sat at the wheel, gazing through the empty windscreen and feeling more at ease with every yard that took them away from the stream where they had made their fatal halt. He was beginning to believe that they were going to reach Sakinda after all.

Then abruptly a lone warrior straightened up form a low tangle of brush to the left of the trail, a brand new automatic rifle held fast in his black hands. He was less than four yards away and his first burst of fire crashed straight into the cab and hit Spencer full in the temple, killing him instantly.

Spencer slumped over the wheel and his weight dragged it to one side. The ambulance swerved out of control and plunged down a slight incline into the bush. It stopped with a shuddering crash as the bonnet ploughed into the thick bole of a giant acacia.

The coldly familiar sound of Bantu war cries shrilled through the heat scorched air.

A Running Fight

Rona Waring screamed as the ambulance careered off the road, and then the scream died to a strangled gasp as the force of the crash threw Canning on top of her, his elbow driving solidly into her stomach. His head had cracked on the lower bed as he went down and for a moment he lay stunned. Then the cries of the Bantu reached his ears and he knew exactly what had happened. The black soldiers of Katanga had cut across country to head him off.

Canning cursed as he struggled to his feet, hardly realising that his spread hand was thrusting down hard on the nurse's breast as he pushed himself upright. Then his sense of touch recognised the soft, curving shape beneath his fingers and in the same moment Rona uttered a short, gasping, 'Oh!' He looked down into her shock-widened eyes and was suddenly sure that the exclamation was more indignant than hurt. Blast it, he thought, touching an officer. Swearing and touching a female officer — she'll probably court martial me.

But it was only a fleeting thought. The ambulance was tilted over at a dangerous angle and already he could hear the Bantu running through the short scrub down the slight incline from the road, shrieking hideously as they closed in. He scooped up his sten gun as the first black fingers scrambled at the rear doors and then he kicked the doors open to meet them.

The edge of the heavy steel door caught the nearest warrior full in the face, sending him flying backwards into the bush. Two others halted only yards away, howling with rage and clumsily aiming the unaccustomed rifles in their hands. Canning fired a hip burst that took both warriors low in the stomach before they could fire. The rest of the Bantu were swarming along the road and he checked their advance with a second sweeping burst from the sten.

He turned hastily and slammed the

doors of the ambulance.

'Bolt them from the inside,' he roared. And without waiting to see whether she obeyed he ran for the cab.

He knew from the abrupt manner in which the ambulance had spun out of control that Spencer must have been hit by the first burst of firing, and he was grimly prepared to find his friend dead or wounded. He steeled his nerves as he pulled open the cab door, but even then they almost failed him. Spencer slumped forwards over the wheel, his face was obliterated by blood where the bullet had entered his temple and the back of his head had torn away around the exit hole.

Then the Bantu uttered another series of hideous war whoops and Canning turned with pure savagery in his heart to direct another stream of chattering fire up the gradual hillside to the road. Then he pulled himself swiftly into the cab.

He hesitated before he could bring himself to touch Spencer, but necessity gave him strength and he pushed the limp body away from the wheel. He had to lift the legs away from the foot pedals and push them to one side. When he straightened up again a dozen warriors were streaming through the bush towards him. The stinging whine of metal tearing across metal echoed insanely in his ears as their bullets ricocheted off the already badly scarred vehicle, but when he thrust his own sten through the side window to fire another burst the Katangans promptly dropped flat in the scrub. They were at last learning that the white soldiers were far more efficient with the new automatic weapons than they were themselves.

Canning rammed the gear lever into neutral and started the engine with one hand. Again the engine fired first time, despite the crumpled bonnet, and Canning offered a thankful prayer to the army mechanic who had kept her so well serviced. He dropped his sten gun across his lap and swiftly put the gears into reverse. He put his foot down and the wheels simply spun. For one horrible second Canning was almost sick with despair, and in desperation he stamped the pedal fully down. The ambulance tore free with a snarling roar, the wheels biting on the crushed branches of the scrub bushes as she backed away from the great acacia that had stopped her downward progress. The handful of warriors who had come up behind the ambulance scattered form its path in the very act of reaching for the doors.

The ambulance tilted even more dangerously as Canning reversed, seeming to hover on the very point of balance where at any moment it could come crashing down on one side. Canning knew he would never back her up the hill and he tried not to think of the agony he must be causing the wounded men in the back as he braked to a jerking stop and then pulled forwards again. He had to wrench the wheel hard round on full lock to miss the torn and bruised trunk of the giant acacia and again there was a horrible moment when he thought that the ambulance must turn completely over. Then mercifully the vehicle straightened up again and he was ploughing through the miniature scrub bushes parallel to the road.

The Bantu were quick to take advantage of the fact that Canning could not possibly control the ambulance and use his sten at the same time, and almost immediately they were on their feet and attacking again. They were only a small fraction of the main force, and Canning guessed that their leaders had not considered it necessary to send the full pack chasing across the country after one vehicle. These two dozen warriors would have been plenty if the attack had been better planned. It was only the fact that the first three or four warriors had opened fire before their companions were in a position to support them that had enabled Canning to reach the cab.

Canning kept his head low, driving blindly and trusting to luck. There were no more large trees near his path and he could only pray that the ambulance would not settle down in the soft earth. For the moment the thick, stumpy bushes were providing a grip for the wheels but at any moment they could run into a patch of clear sand. Bullets clanged repeatedly off the ambulance's sides and a neatly thrown spear sailed clean through the side window of the cab, the broad blade smashed into the inside of the opposite door frame and the hardwood shaft smacked heavily on Canning's bowed shoulders as it fell.

Canning risked a quick glance to see where he was going and saw that he was almost past the main party of warriors who were still spread out on the slope leading up to the Sakinda road on his right-hand side. Most of them had stopped running now and were firing excitedly but with little effect. Then he saw three screaming blacks rushing towards him, ahead of the ambulance and slightly right of its path. Two of them carried primitive bows and the third wildly waved a rifle, and two out of the three were wearing blue United Nations berets on their curly heads; berets that were soiled with purple-red bloodstains. Canning realised then for the first time that several of their attackers were wearing army shirts or battle blouses, clothing that could only have been taken from the bodies of the men killed at the stream.

The realisation that Holland's detachment must have been completely wiped out kindled blind fury in Canning's heart and he swung the wheel savagely to the right. The three warriors tried to scatter but they were much too slow. Canning used the heavy ambulance as a bull-dozer to plough them into the earth, cursing crazily as he crushed them beneath the lumbering wheels. He swung the ambulance back on to its path again and now the way was clear ahead. Then he heard Rona Waring scream.

Rona had been unable to get the back doors of the ambulance properly closed and with the sudden swerve that Canning had made to drive into the three warriors one of the double doors had sprung wide open. Instantly the milling Bantu had taken up the pursuit again and within seconds the leading warrior had leaped into the back of the ambulance with a beautifully athletic spring. That was when Rona had screamed.

Canning looked back through the communication panel and realised what had happened. But for once he was

116

completely helpless and without stopping the ambulance there was nothing he could do. Even if he could have got the snout of his sten through the open slit. Rona would still be between him and the triumphant negro.

The Bantu was a big man for his race, a young warrior at the peak of physical fitness. He had lost his loin cloth as he raced through the bush and he was naked but for a bloodstained army jacket that adorned his shoulders. His black muscles glistened with sweat and both his face and chest had been covered by primitive tattoo marks. He had already thrown his spear and now he crouched with only a knife. His eyes had the widened stare of a madman, and there was an insanely happy grin on his face as he realised that he had only one terror-frozen woman to deal with. He uttered a shrieking cry, sprang over the inert bodies of Baxter and Delayney, and lunged with the knife.

A hand heaved at Rona's shoulder and pulled her backwards. The knife missed but instantly flashed again. Ginger Morris swayed drunkenly on his feet, he had pulled himself up as he dragged the nurse back and now he released her and grabbed desperately at the black wrist with his one hand. He fell forwards at the same time and his weight dragged the Bantu's knife hand downwards. His head wound was throbbing furiously and with his other arm completely useless there was only one thing left that he could do. He sank his teeth into the black forearm and bit as hard as his jaw could contract.

Rona Waring was spread-eagled against the back wall of the ambulance, half-standing and half-lying as she stared in horror at the little man clinging like a terrier to the Bantu's wrist. The big black howled with pain and aimed a clumsy blow at Morris's head. The sight released a last reserve of courage that flooded through Rona's limbs and she hurled herself bodily at the struggling warrior, grabbing at his free arm with both hands.

The Bantu staggered but remained upright, and for a moment all three wrestled desperately in the back of the speeding ambulance. Morris hung on doggedly, incapable of doing any more than keep his teeth buried in the black man's arm. Then Rona lost her grip and the Bantu's free arm wrapped instantly around her waist, crushing her to his naked body in an agonising lover's embrace. Rona screamed again, arching her shoulders backwards and twisting her face away from the contorted features looming above her. The smell of him made her sick and the very touch of his bare flesh sent shudders of revulsion through her body. Then with a final effort the Bantu shook the weakening Morris away and his right hand, now empty, closed around her throat.

Triumph gleamed in the warrior's eyes again, but there was still one other man in the ambulance who had retained consciousness. Morris's efforts had been short-lived, but at least they had given Baxter time to twist his body round and grope for the sten that lay beside him on the floor. Baxter had taken his time in aiming the gun, for with the ambulance throwing them all from side to side as it crashed over the rough ground he could easily have hit the wrong target in the mêlée of flailing limbs. But now that Morris had fallen away and Rona was arching backwards in the native's grasp Baxter had a clear shot. He angled the sten upwards, squeezed the trigger for a fraction of a second and shot the back of the man's head off. The half-spent bullet carried on to deflect off the inside of the roof and then bury itself in Garner's pillow.

In the front of the ambulance Canning heard the shot and breathed a sigh of relief as he saw the Katangan fall away. Rona stood swaying for a moment and then collapsed in a dead faint, but Canning could see no more for he had to turn his head away to control the ambulance.

There were still two or three warriors running behind the ambulance, but they were hampered by the tangled vegetation and were gradually falling behind. The real danger came from the main party who had scrambled back up the slope and who were now easily keeping pace with the ambulance as they ran along the open road. Every few moments they would stop to fire their bows and rifles down the slope.

The terrain was so rough that it was impossible for Canning to get any real speed out of the ambulance, and the gradual slope was still too steep for him to regain the road. He could only drive on and pray.

For almost a mile the running Bantu kept pace with the ambulance, and with every yard Canning was tensed to meet the disaster of a broken axle or the wheels spinning themselves to a standstill in the soft sand. He kept his head down below the metal-work of the cab as much as possible, but fortunately the negroes had exhausted their spears and arrows and they were very poor shots with their new rifles.

Then gradually the ambulance began to pull ahead and the level of the road dropped until Canning was able to swing right and steer back on to it. The moment he was clear of the low bushes and grassland he was able to move up a gear and leave the Bantu far behind again as he drove hard for Sakinda.

He drove on until he was confident that he had put several miles between himself and his pursuers and then he stopped the ambulance. For a moment he sat rigidly at the wheel, soaked in sweat and trembling from a delayed reaction of nausea that twisted in his stomach. Then unwillingly his eyes were drawn to the body of Spencer slumped in the cab beside him. He and Roy Spencer had shared this cab for a long time and had become good friends. It was hard to believe that Spencer was dead. At last he shook his head helplessly from side to side and told himself grimly that there was nothing he could do for Spencer now. His job was to take care of the wounded in his charge.

He picked up his sten which still lay across his knees, for nothing would induce him to move about unarmed now, and wearily he got down from the cab. One of the double doors still swung open and he climbed slowly inside.

Baxter was lying on his back with his sten held tight against his chest, he was still defiantly conscious but his eyes were closed against the pain from his foot. The dead negro had fallen across Delayney's legs, sprawling obscenely with his sightless eyes staring up at the roof. Rona Waring huddled on the floor, sobbing brokenly beside him. While Morris crouched at the end of the ambulance with the Bantu's knife held limply in his one hand. He looked at Canning but said nothing.

Canning looked at Hardman and saw to his relief that the big Sergeant was still alive, although in very poor shape. Jack Foster lay very still on the opposite bed and slowly Canning realised that he was dead. The vicious jolting as he had forced the ambulance over the rough ground had caused a haemorrhage.

Slowly Canning moved farther into the ambulance. Morris laid down his knife and settled back on his haunches to nurse his bandaged arm. He started to say something then changed his mind and looked helplessly at Rona. Her shuddering sobs were the only sounds that broke the unnatural silence.

Canning put down his sten gun without

speaking and turned to the body of the Bantu. With an effort he lifted the dead man from Delayney's legs and carried him out of the ambulance, staggering slightly as he dropped on to the road. He dumped the body on the edge of the track and stared down at it for a moment, his fists knotted at the sight of the soiled army jacket that the man was wearing. Then he went back to the ambulance.

He instinctively picked up his sten again as he climbed inside, and then he moved over to Rona. She still huddled on the floor, crying wretchedly. For the first time Canning was unable to resent her rank as he said quietly: 'Lieutenant.'

She didn't look up and he had to repeat the word in a louder tone. He knelt and gripped her arm to steady her and then slowly she turned a tear-stained face towards him. Her eyes were dull and her mouth quivered uncontrollably.

Canning said, 'You'd better let me help you outside.'

She made no protest, no resistance as he pulled her upright with one hand,

and still gripping her arm Canning led her over to the open doors. There she stopped, unwilling to move any farther. Her mouth trembled again and she said dully:

'He's dead.'

For a moment Canning didn't understand. He looked at Foster lying motionless on his bed and said quietly:

'It couldn't be helped. He would probably have died anyway.'

But Rona wasn't looking at Foster, she was staring at the black corpse Canning had left on the edge of the road only a few yards away.

'He's dead,' she said again. 'Jimmy's dead.'

Canning still didn't understand. Then he followed the direction of her gaze towards the dead warrior and understanding became savagely clear. The army jacket that the man wore was horribly blood-stained and pierced in a dozen places with ragged tears that could only have been made by knife or spear thrusts, but the right shoulder still bore the rank markings of a Lieutenant of the

British army. The jacket was Holland's.

Canning stepped down on to the road and pulled Rona down beside him. She leaned helplessly with her shoulders pressed back against the open door of the ambulance and stared past him with blank, unseeing eyes.

Canning said, 'I'm sorry, Lieutenant.'

His voice penetrated and her eyes focused slowly on his face. 'Jimmy's dead,' she repeated. 'They killed him.' Her voice became hysterical, 'They killed them all.'

'Take it easy, Lieutenant.'

She said wildly, 'They're all dead. Don't you understand! They're all dead!' Her whole body was shaking now and her voice rose to a scream. 'Jimmy's dead and they'll kill us next. They'll catch us and kill us.'

Canning shook her sharply. 'For Christ's sake control yourself.'

It was a mistake, for the violent shaking sent her completely hysterical. She tore blindly free from Canning's grip, striking out at his face as she tried to run. She stumbled and almost fell and then Canning caught her again, fastening his fingers cruelly on her shoulder. She struggled in insane frenzy, kicking and clawing as he fought to restrain her. Hysteria gave her a writhing, squirming strength and Canning found it almost impossible to hold her. She was both sobbing and screaming at the same time.

'We're all going to die. Can't you understand? They'll catch us again and there's only you against hundreds of them. We're all going to die. They'll never let us go.'

Canning's control snapped and he spun her around to slam her shoulders hard against the open door of the ambulance. The impact drove the breath from her lungs and then the back of his hand stung her hard across the face. She uttered a shuddering gasp and then his hand locked on the lapel of her blouse and twisted, tearing the buttons open as he pressed her against the door. For a moment there was fear in her eyes and then he shook his sten, still clamped in his left fist, within inches of her face.

'Nobody's going to die,' he said savagely. 'Do you hear me! Nobody. I'm taking this ambulance back to Sakinda with everyone in it alive — and nothing this side of hell is going to stop me!'

A Trial of Strength

For a long moment the heavy panting of their breathing was the only sound beside the stationary ambulance. Then slowly Canning lowered his sten gun to his side. His right hand was still fastened on the edge of her open blouse and her full breasts heaved jerkily against the half cups of her bra. The soft whiteness of her skin glistened with tiny globes of sweat above the black lace. Her whole body was trembling but slowly, infinitely slowly, she relaxed and let the tension seep out of her muscles. Her mouth was slightly open, the lips quivering, and her blue eyes were blank and distended, but slowly the traces of hysteria began to fade.

She said, 'I — I'm sorry, Corporal.'

She pulled herself together and looked down at her gaping blouse. Hesitantly she put her hand on his wrist and pushed it away. Canning released her and stepped back a pace.

129

He said quietly, 'We'll be back at Sakinda before nightfall. It's very unlikely that the Bantu will be able to head us off again.'

Rona met his eyes for a moment and then looked down, lowering her gaze to the level of his chin.

'I'm sorry,' she repeated. It was all she could think of to say.

Canning was at a loss for an answer. He wanted to say something gentle but he could not bring himself to speak. The stubborn savagery that had gripped him a moment ago, like her hysteria, had faded away. Then he heard a movement from just inside the ambulance.

Morris stood there, a battered and uncertain little figure, his eyes troubled beneath the heavy bandage that obscured all but a few unruly strands of his ginger hair. He had picked up Baxter's sten and now it hung limply in his one hand.

'Is everything all right, Corp?' he asked.

Canning said, 'It is now.'

Rona Waring's fingers moved to button up her blouse, fumbling clumsily before the realisation came that the buttons had been torn away. She faltered, and then tucked the two sides of the blouse tighter into the top of her skirt to bring the edges together. Then she straightened herself up and tried to instil a note of authority into her voice as she spoke to Morris:

'You're not fit enough to be up. You should be in bed.'

Morris looked at her in surprise. 'I haven't got a bed,' he reminded her.

The conversation sounded unreal, and Canning realised that Rona's mind was still groping slightly as she struggled to re-orientate her thoughts. He put a hand on her shoulder, gently this time, and said:

'You'd better sit down for a minute, Lieutenant. Just relax in the shade. I've got a couple of jobs to do before we can drive on.'

Morris said vaguely, 'Can I help, Corp?'

Canning shook his head, 'I can manage.' Then he paused and changed his mind. 'Someone ought to get up on the roof and keep watch. Can you do that if I help you to climb up?'

Before Morris could answer Rona said stiffly, 'He — he isn't fit. I'll keep watch for you.'

Canning started to voice a protest, then stopped it. The task would give her something to do, it would divert her attention from his own movements while he buried Spencer and Foster, and most of all, it might help to take her mind off Holland. Then with a sudden shock, he realised that he had thought exactly the same thing about Spencer; he had given his friend a job to occupy his mind, and Spencer had died in his place at the wheel of the ambulance.

However, Rona had already taken the sten gun from Morris's reluctant hand. She was still trembling slightly, but she had recovered most of her courage and her voice was steady. She said to Morris:

'Perhaps you can keep watch on Private Garner for me. If he starts to twist about in his fever give me a shout.'

'Yes, Ma'am,' Morris nodded vaguely, 'I can do that.'

132

Rona turned away and Canning followed her up to the front of the ambulance. For the second time he put his hand on her shoulder to stop her, causing her to turn her head uncertainly.

He said quietly, 'Try not to look in the cab, Lieutenant.'

She hesitated and the soft whiteness of her throat moved convulsively in an involuntary swallowing motion. Then she said slowly:

'It's all right, Corporal. I won't get hysterical again.'

Canning nodded, and then helped her to climb up over the cab. She tried to prevent her gaze from being drawn inside, but it was impossible, and when she saw Spencer her face whitened and a shudder ran through the upper half of her body. Canning knew that at least his warning had prepared her for what she could not have failed to see, and he hurried her on to the roof as fast as he could. She stayed there on her knees for a moment, and then he passed her Baxter's sten gun.

'Watch the back trial,' he said. 'The

country is fairly open so you should be able to spot any sign of pursuit in good time.'

She nodded, straightened up, and stared rigidly down the dusty road towards Kasuvu. Canning returned to the back of the ambulance.

He found that Hardman was conscious again. The big Sergeant still lay motionless, but his eyes were open, and only the twisted set of his face hinted at the pain he was suffering. Despite the fact that he was completely immobilised Hardman was still aware of his rank, and at the moment his mind was as clear as any man's could have possibly been in his critical condition.

He said feebly, 'Where are we, Corporal? What's happening?'

Canning had not expected the big man to remain alive as long as this, much less to recover consciousness, but he kept his thoughts to himself as he answered.

'We've covered just over half the distance back to Sakinda, and we've beaten off a second attack by some of the Bantu who got ahead of us. Both

134

Foster and my co-driver are dead, and as soon as I've buried them we'll drive on to Sakinda. We should make it without any more trouble.'

Hardman said slowly, 'What about the rest of the men; those left behind at the stream?'

Canning was aware that both Baxter and Morris were listening intently, and he wished that Hardman had not asked that question. Baxter's eyes were closed, but Morris was standing by Garner's bed and staring nervously The flash of courage that Morris had shown in protecting Rona Waring had died with the heat of the moment, and now he looked rather untidy and insignificant.

Canning said at last, 'I don't think there's any hope for them, Sergeant. Several of the tribesmen who attacked us the second time were wearing scraps of army uniforms, and that's a pretty bad sign.'

Hardman was silent for a moment. Then he said, 'Don't waste time burying the bodies, Corporal. You'd better take them back to Sakinda.'

'We've got the time.' Canning's voice was toneless. 'The radiator's boiling after that last run through the bush so I'll have to wait for it to cool. Besides, the ambulance is already overloaded and I need Foster's bed for Delayney.'

Hardman didn't argue, but he was still heavily conscious of the fact that he was still the Sergeant, and still carried a sergeant's responsibilities. He said:

'Make it as quick as you can, Corporal. We're not really safe until we get back to Sakinda.'

Canning nodded, and then turned to Morris:

'Give me a shout if I'm needed in here,' he said briefly. And then he turned away.

He untied the shovel that was part of the ambulance's equipment and moved a few paces into the bush. He found a clear space between some of the low wait-a-bit thorns and began to dig.

It was a hot, exhausting work beneath a pitiless sun. The sand was dry as powder and trickled back into the shallow trench he made almost as fast as he shovelled it out. He sweated freely and his shirt stuck uncomfortably to his back. At last the irritation of the shirt became too much and he pulled it off and worked stripped to the waist. His back and shoulders were already bronzed and he knew that he could quite safely work for half an hour or more without burning.

It took him fifteen minutes to dig a wide trench some two foot deep and six long, and into this he laid Spencer and Foster side by side on a blanket. He used a second blanket to spread over them and then grimly re-filled the hole. Finally he hunted about the scrub for rocks until he had found enough to build a low mound over the twin grave. He knew that a party would eventually be sent out from Sakinda to recover the bodies for a proper military burial, but until then they would be safe from the scavenging jackals and hyenas that roamed the jungle. A flock of vultures watching from the tall branches of some nearby trees eyed him with malignant hatred as he placed the last few rocks in position.

He picked up his shirt and the shovel

and returned to the ambulance, swearing as the vicious wait-a-bit thorns caught at his legs. He had to pluck them carefully away before he could step back on to the road. Rona Waring heard him approach and looked down at him from the roof of the ambulance.

Canning met her eyes, and wondered dully whether there was any army law against appearing half-dressed before a female officer. But he didn't know and he didn't care. He said:

'The job's finished, and the engine should be cool enough for us to drive on. You can come down now.'

She climbed down slowly, but apart from taking the sten gun she handed him he made no move to help her. She straightened up to face him as she reached the ground and then he said:

'I want to lift Delayney on to Foster's bed. Will you give me a hand?'

'Of course.' There was resentment, almost hurt, in her tone. 'It's my job isn't it?'

Canning knew that his tone had been unnecessarily harsh, but although he almost immediately regretted it he was unable to apologise. He hesitated for a moment and then Rona lowered her gaze from his face and went to the back of the ambulance. Canning replaced his shovel and pulled his shirt back on to his shoulders. Then, still feeling guilty, he followed her.

Rona was already kneeling between Delayney and Baxter, and Canning saw that Delayney had also recovered consciousness. The wounded man twisted his head as he heard Canning enter and asked weakly:

'What happened to my sten, Corp? What happened to it?'

'Don't worry about it.' Canning knelt beside him. 'The Bantu are a long way behind us so I don't think you'll need it again.'

Delayney relaxed, then he looked up again and grinned faintly, 'Did I get many, Corp? Before I passed out — did I get many?'

'You got a few. How are you feeling now?'

'Bloody awful.' Delayney was still

grinning, but his teeth were tightly clenched.

Canning said, 'We're going to lift you on to the bed, you'll be more comfortable there. Do you think you can take it?'

Delayney's grin narrowed a fraction, 'There were no beds when we started. What's happened?'

'Jack Foster died.' Canning tried to keep the bitterness out of his voice.

Delayney was silent for a moment. Then he grinned again:

'Might have known it wouldn't be that bastard Hardman. That's too much to hope for.'

Rona said curtly: 'That's enough.' She looked at Canning: 'Are you ready?'

Canning nodded, 'I'll lift him, you steady his shoulders.' He slid one arm underneath Delayney's waist and the other beneath the man's thighs. Then he lifted as gently as he could. Delayney's grin vanished as his mouth tightened with pain. His whole body stiffened in Canning's arms. Then, with Rona supporting his head and shoulders, and Morris steadying the legs with his one arm, Canning laid the man carefully on the bed that had carried the unfortunate Foster. They stepped back and Rona used a square of cloth to clean the sweat from the sick man's temples, and over a minute passed before the stiffness began to relax from his frame. At last his eyes opened again and he said weakly:

'That hurt!'

Rona said quietly, 'I know. But once we get to Sakinda we'll get a helicopter to fly you out. You'll soon be getting proper attention in hospital.'

Delayney gave her another ragged grin, and then closed his eyes once more.

They turned to Baxter and used some of the pillows that had been packed round Delayney to make the tall man more comfortable on the floor. When they had finished Baxter smiled at Rona and said briefly:

'Thank you, Ma'am. Now if you can just lay my sten within reach again I shall be quite happy.'

Rona hesitated, but Canning did as Baxter asked. He remembered the long warrior who had leaped into the ambulance to attack Rona, and he knew that if the sten was to be needed again, then Baxter was the most reliable man to use it.

Finally Canning picked up his own sten and looked at Rona.

'If everyone is settled it's time we drove on. Can you manage now, Lieutenant?'

'Perfectly.' Rona smiled, but it was wholly for the benefit of the wounded men. Canning had been unable to instil any respect into the word Lieutenant and the barrier was still there between them. She said coldly, 'Carry on, Corporal.'

Canning closed the doors of the ambulance behind him and returned to his cab. He slammed the door shut and laid his sten close at hand on the seat. Angrily he started the engine and released the brake, and as the vehicle started forward he found himself thinking again of the vivid likeness between Rona and Jenny. And Jenny's memory was like toothache in his brain, a driving, nagging pain that blinded him to everything else.

For several miles he brooded, and then with an effort he pushed Rona

Waring and his ex-fiancée out of his mind, and began to concentrate on his driving. The road was the same, never-ending ribbon of dust stretching through the sun-yellowed heat-blasted bush, and the sun, although now on the downward climb, was still high in the western sky.

Canning drove steadily, mindful of the injured men in the back, and reasonably confident that he had nothing more to fear from the Bantu. The black soldiers of Katanga had made one attempt to head him off and had been repulsed, and he doubted whether they would try again.

His arms and shoulders were aching now and he was beginning to feel the strain of long hours of action and driving. The overpowering heat made everything an effort, and now that Sakinda and safety were drawing steadily nearer he could feel a strong temptation to allow weariness to take over. Many times he glanced at the empty seat beside him, and felt a tightening constriction in his throat, coupled with a cold and strangely empty feeling in his stomach. Spencer's death had affected him more than the slaughter at the scene of the ambush; partly because Spencer had been his closest friend, and partly because although the men at the stream could be pushed into the back of his mind Spencer could not be dismissed so easily. Roy Spencer had been part of the ambulance, and the silent, empty cab was a permanent reminder of his absence.

Canning could not keep his mind away from that empty seat in the cab beside him, and every few moments his eyes would be drawn away from the road into that blank space where Spencer should have been sitting. It was as though, even though he had buried his friend, he could not quite believe that Spencer was gone.

And it was in one of those moments, when he turned to glance at Spencer's seat, that he ran straight into the mud hole.

In the rainy season it was obviously a fair-sized water hole, but now it was half dried up and mostly mud. The road curved round it, and when the convoy had passed early that morning each vehicle had been keeping well to the left and had got by without any difficulty. Now, from force of habit, Canning was again keeping well left, and not until the sunbaked crust broke away and dropped the heavy ambulance into the mud beneath did he realise what was happening. Desperately he heaved on the wheel to bring the ambulance back on to the road, and the front wheels pulled free with a repulsive sucking noise as he thrust his foot hard down. For a moment he thought he had pulled clear in time, and then the back end of the ambulance skidded into the mud and slowly began to settle down as the wheels spun helplessly.

Canning knew that it was useless to spin the wheels any deeper and wearily stopped the engine. For once he didn't swear, for he was at last learning the futility of swearing when things went wrong. He got down from the cab and walked back to appraise the situation.

The whole mud hole covered a large, circular area by the side of the road, surrounded by dense thickets of thorn-bush. In the centre of the circle was a small amount of filthy black water, and the mud immediately around it had been churned and trampled by the pawing feet of the animals who made regular nocturnal visits. Nearer the edge the mud was baked hard by the sun, and here the rear wheels of the ambulance had embedded themselves up to the axle.

Canning stared at them bitterly, and then the rear doors of the ambulance were pushed open from the inside. Canning walked forward and pulled the door back as Rona Waring stepped down on to the mud. She looked at him without expression. 'Well, Corporal. What now?'

There was a note of rebuke in her voice that made Caning's stubborn streak show through again.

He said grimly, 'We dig the damned thing out, Lieutenant. We just dig the damned thing out.'

He started to turn away and then Hardman called to him with a note of weak authority. Slowly he moved closer to the ambulance and met the sick man's eyes.

'Yes, Sergeant!'

Hardman said, 'I take it that we're in the mud hole we passed on the way out this morning. How bad is it?'

'The front wheels are clear, but the back is bogged down to the axle.'

Hardman grimaced, 'When you've dug the wheels out cut plenty of branches and bush to throw down in front of them. You'll never pull out unless you give the tyres something to grip.'

Canning had already thought of that, but he felt no resentment now towards the big Sergeant. Instead he felt strengthened by the knowledge that Hardman's trained mind was there to cover anything he might have missed.

He said, 'Thanks, Sergeant. I'll do that.'

Hardman nodded, his big jaw jerking in a gesture of acknowledgement. Then his head sank back upon his pillow. Rona looked at him with worried eyes and then turned to Canning:

'I'll gather the branches,' she offered, 'while you do the digging.'

Canning felt too tired to answer. He pulled off his shirt and took down his shovel for the second time in just over an hour. Rona watched him start to dig at the mud around the bogged wheels and then moved into the bush to gather branches. The sun still blazed fiercely and Canning wondered how long a man could go on exuding sweat before his body became completely arid. He felt sure that he must be nearing the danger mark.

The thin crust soon broke under his weight and he was working up to his ankles in mud and slowly sinking deeper, and he began to wonder whether it was humanly possible to free the ambulance with his limited resources. Then he consoled himself with the thought that as the vastly heavier ambulance had now stopped sinking any farther its wheels must have touched solid ground, and given time he must be able to drive it out.

Then he began to wonder whether the Bantu would allow him enough time. It was easy to be confident when sitting in the cab with Sakinda drawing ever nearer and the blacks falling farther and farther behind. But now that they were stuck fast in the mud they made a sitting target for any of the Katangans who might still be on the trail. He tried to convince himself that the Bantu must have given up the chase, but now it was impossible to be sure and weariness dropped away from his tiring muscles as determination gave him new strength.

Three times Rona Waring appeared out of the bush with her arms full of broken branches which she threw down beside the ambulance, and after the third trip Canning noticed that her left arm had been badly scratched by the sharp wait-a-bit thorns. Her buttonless blouse had worked loose from the top of her skirt and was again gaping open, but she did not appear to have noticed. Her eyes were dull and her movements sluggish as she turned to go back for the fourth time.

Canning said, 'That should be enough, Lieutenant. Find some shade and take a break.'

She looked back slowly, 'We need as much as we can get.'

'Maybe. But you've got time to take a breather.'

She stared at him for a moment, and suddenly Canning found his gaze drawn irresistably towards her open blouse, realising with a sense of shock that the glistening, swelling breasts in their revealing cups of black lace still had the power to stir him into a vague sense of excitement. Then the memory of Jenny returned to crush the barely conceived tingle to nothing, and in the same moment Rona's eyes hardened and her shoulders stiffened as she caught the direction of his gaze. Fresh energy flooded her fingers as she deftly straightened her blouse, and then she turned quickly into the bush. Canning threw himself savagely into his digging, cursing himself for his own weakness.

When she returned again he had cleared most of the mud away from the trapped wheels, shelving it upwards as best he could to the edge of the mud hole. She dropped the fourth load of branches beside him and without looking up at her he began to weave them into an interlocked carpet before the wheels. The bigger branches he jammed as far underneath as he could, and when he had finished he felt that there was a reasonable chance of the ambulance pulling clear.

He straightened up, wiping the streaks of mud from his bare arms and shoulders, but still refusing to look at her. He wiped the sweat from his temples with the back of his hand and left a smear of black mud in its place, and then he went to the back of the ambulance. Morris was standing upright, watching him.

He said, 'You'd better get out for a bit, chum. I don't suppose you're very heavy, but a few pounds might make all the difference.'

Morris grinned faintly, 'Nine-stone-four, Corp. If that's any help.'

Canning smiled back, 'It might be.' He gave the little man a hand to step out of the ambulance, and then realised that Baxter was looking up at him.

The tall man said, 'If you'll just help me up, I'll hop out too.'

Canning accepted the offer and helped him up on to one leg. He got Baxter's arm over his shoulders and then Rona took the man's other arm and also lifted his injured leg, holding it high so that it could not drag on the floor. Baxter winced and gritted his teeth, but he made no other sound as they lifted him out of the ambulance and laid him on the grass beyond the mud hole.

Canning returned to the ambulance and carried Garner out. When he got back he found Delayney waiting in turn.

Delayney said, 'I guess I can take it too, Corp.'

Canning shook his head, 'Not you — or the Sergeant. At least not until I've had a couple of tries to pull her out first.' He gave them both a grin and then closed the doors and went forwards to his cab.

He started the engine, put the ambulance into first, and slowly released the clutch. The vehicle moved forward with a slight jerk and the branches snapped crisply beneath her weight as she started to pull free. Canning applied a fractional amount of pressure to the accelerator and more branches crunched as the ambulance gained another inch. Gently Canning increased the pressure on the accelerator and then abruptly the wheels began to spin. Savagely Canning stamped his foot hard down. The ambulance lurched forward and mud and twigs sprayed up from the revolving wheels. She seemed to hover on the point of tearing free, and then slowly she began to settle again.

Canning opened his door, leaning out so that he could watch the wheels as he dipped the clutch and allowed the ambulance to roll back. Then he released the clutch and roared the vehicle forward again. The wheels rolled less than six inches and again began to spin. Canning allowed her to go back again, stopped the engine and climbed out.

Rona watched him without speaking and he said simply:

'More branches.'

Together they moved into the bush and gathered more of the broken branches. Canning selected the thickest ones he could find and these he jammed directly beneath the wheels, building a near solid ramp almost to the edge of the mud hole. Then he again climbed into the cab and warned Rona and Morris to stand well clear.

Canning started the engine and leaned out again so that he could see the rear wheel. He put the ambulance into first and flattened his foot on the floorboards. The vehicle seemed to leap forward and for a moment it seemed that the wheels must mount the ramp of branches. Then the ambulance sagged backwards and the wheels spun again on the edge of the ramp. The engine roared under Canning's thrusting foot but to no avail. The ambulance was stuck as firmly as ever.

Canning stopped revving the engine and put the gear into neutral. Wearily he got down from the cab.

Rona came closer and when she spoke there was defeat in her voice, 'You'll never get her out of there,' she said dully. 'You need another lorry at least to give you a pull.'

Canning's stubbornness returned. He remembered his violent promise to get them all back to Sakinda, and he was determined not to give up at this early stage. He said flatly:

'Can you drive?'

She looked at him without understanding, 'Yes. Why?'

He gestured to the cab, 'Get in there and put your foot down. Just keep it down while I give her a push.'

For a moment he thought she was going to argue, but then she climbed obediently into the cab. She settled herself into the driving seat and looked down at him:

'Tell me when you're ready.'

Canning nodded and waded out into the mud hole to the back of the ambulance. He was again in mud several inches past his ankles but he ignored it and braced his shoulder against the ambulance. Then he raised his voice and shouted.

Almost immediately Rona put her foot down. The ambulance lurched and Canning thrust with it. Then the wheels rubbed on the edge of the ramp again and began to spin. Canning strained every muscle as he hurled all his

155

weight repeatedly against the back of the ambulance but the vehicle refused to budge. Mud sprayed up from the whirling wheels and spattered Canning from head to toe. Flying branches smacked into his legs and then his feet slowly slithered backwards in the mud. Then abruptly Rona relaxed her foot on the pedal and the ambulance rolled back. Canning slipped to his knees and swore as a flying clod of mud stung him wetly across the side of his neck.

Rona put her foot down for the second time and the ambulance jolted back to the edge of the ramp. Canning found his balance and threw his weight back into the struggle, straining until every muscle ached and screamed for release. Mud covered him from the spraying wheels and the harsh reverberating of the engine snarled in the still air. Canning was suddenly and horribly aware that the roaring of their engine would attract every warrior for miles, and the new fear gave him added strength. Then again Rona allowed the ambulance to roll back and the roaring stopped.

Canning gasped for breath, and then realised that she had climbed down from the cab and was standing on the edge of the mud hole and staring at him.

She said helplessly, 'It's no good, Corporal. It's no good. She just won't move.'

'Get back in the cab.' Canning's voice was cold with barely suppressed fury. 'Get back in that bloody cab and keep your bloody foot down. Keep it down until I tell you to stop.'

A look of shocked indignation sparked in her eyes, and for a moment she was too stunned to answer.

Cannning repeated savagely, '*Get back in that Bloody cab!*'

Rona stared at him for a second and then turned back to the cab.

Canning waited until the engine roared and the ambulance lurched forward again, and then he threw everything he had into one last demented, muscle-tearing effort. The blazing sun seared the aching muscles in his naked back and the sweat gummed his eyes together as he pushed in blind fury. The mud rained up into his face and chest and he gritted his teeth against the fresh barrage of broken branches that were hurled back against his braced legs. Then slowly and inexorably his feet began to slide backwards, and in the same moment he felt the ambulance move fractionally forwards. Every sinew tightened to the utmost as he made the final titanic effort and his feet slithered farther back in the mud. Then there was a sudden, ripping, squelching sound as the wheels lifted out of the clinging slime and balanced precariously on the edge of the ramp. Canning was already falling as the ambulance burst free and churned up the ramp, and then he sprawled face down in the mud.

Aftermath of Murder

Exhaustion held Canning fast in the mud hole, pinning him down like a solid weight on his shoulders. His mouth and nostrils were pressed hard into the oozing mire and he choked helplessly as he tried to breathe. He felt the horrible fear of suffocation sweep through him, and that fear threw up the last few dregs of strength to enable him to roll over on to his back. He lay there, panting hoarsely, and vaguely aware that the sound of the ambulance's engine had stopped. He sensed a movement beside him, but the plastered muck over his tightly closed eyes had rendered him temporarily blind.

His head was lifted and supported clear of the mud, and then the slime was wiped from his eyes. After a moment he was able to open his lids and look upwards. Rona Waring was kneeling in the mud hole behind him with his head resting in the lap of her skirt. She used the piece of torn sheet in her hand to clean more of the wet mud from his face and said quietly:

'Are you all right, Corporal?'

He tried to move his head but lacked the strength. Finally he said, 'I will be, once I get my breath back.'

There was a shuffling sound from the edge of the mud hole. Morris stood there, his good arm hugging the wounded one to his chest.

'Is there anything I can do, Ma'am?'

In the same moment they heard Hardman calling weakly.

Rona said, 'You can get back in the ambulance and tell the men inside that everything is all right, and that we'll be driving on in a few minutes.'

'Yes, Ma'am.' Morris turned to do as he was asked.

Rona looked down at Canning. 'Just relax for five minutes, Corporal. We've got plenty of time.'

Canning refused. If she had left him lying alone in the mud he could willingly have stayed there for an hour, but the physical contact as his head rested between her thighs brought back a stark mental picture of Jenny. His ex-fiancée had often cradled his head on her lap as they relaxed on the floor of the flat in Kensington, and now nothing would induce him to remain in that same position again. He struggled stubbornly to his feet, ignoring the expression of baffled anger that appeared on her face. She sensed his antagonism and stepped away as soon as he was standing upright. Once the contact was broken he couldn't avoid the uncomprehending blue of her eyes and his resentment was touched with guilt once more.

'We haven't got time,' he excused himself awkwardly. 'The Bantu might have been near enough to hear our engine roaring. They could turn up at any moment.'

Rona didn't answer, the expression in her eyes hadn't changed and he knew the explanation had been unconvincing. He turned away and stumbled deeper into the mud hole to the stirred-up pool of unclean water. The water was lukewarm, but at least it washed off the thickest of the mud and helped to revive him. When he returned to the ambulance she proffered his shirt without speaking.

Canning said, 'thank you,' clumsily. And then he avoided her eyes as she watched him don the shirt. Together they lifted Garner and Baxter back into the ambulance, and then Canning returned his shovel to its place. When he turned away Rona was facing him.

She said, 'You can take a rest, Corporal. I'll drive.'

Canning said flatly, 'I'm driving.'

Her eyes didn't falter, 'I could make that an order.'

Canning gave her a hard look, but when he spoke he found his voice was strangely calm. 'You could, Lieutenant. But I'd ignore it. When we're all safe and happy in Sakinda, then you can start acting your rank again. But until then I'm in charge of this ambulance and I'll give the orders. You'll ride in the back and take care of the patients, and I'll do the driving.'

For several seconds she stared into

the stubborn lines of his face and the unyielding grey of his eyes. Then she said slowly:

'Corporal, you've had a grudge against me ever since we met. I don't know why and I don't care. But I do know that I can have you court martialled for this. I'll think about it when we get back to Sakinda.'

Then she turned coldly away and climbed into the back of the ambulance. Canning closed the doors behind her and went back to his cab.

Soon the mud hole was left behind them and they were swallowed up by scrub and bush. The thickets were getting denser and crowding in to overhang the road, the thorns and branches raking at the bullet-scarred sides of the ambulance. Canning kept his eyes fixed firmly on the road ahead, forcing Spencer and everything else from his mind in his determination not to make any more mistakes. He felt strangely subdued now that he had openly rebelled against Rona's authority, and he wondered sourly whether the satisfaction he had achieved

163

was really worth a court martial.

The miles rolled past, swirling into the dust clouds behind them. It was late afternoon but the cab still retained the heat like an airless oven, even with the windscreen gone there was hardly any draught. There was an occasional murmer of voices from the back of the ambulance; an occasional jolt as the wheels hit a gulley. It was a long time since dawn and Canning could feel the first, sharp tugs of hunger below his belt. For hours he had tasted nothing but dust and the thought of water became a longing torment. He pushed the thought wearily away and told himself that it could not be many more miles to Sakinda. They must be nearly there by now.

And then, two miles from Sakinda, the ambulance spluttered to a sudden, totally unexpected stop.

Canning recognised the choking protest of a starved engine and looked down with a sense of unbelieving despair. Theoretically there should have been plenty of petrol, for the tanks had been filled to capacity before they left Sakinda, but the strangled voice of the engine had not lied. The ambulance spluttered once more and then the engine died altogether. In silence the still-moving wheels rolled a last few ponderous yards before coming to rest. The white needle on the fuel gauge registered an emphatic zero.

For a moment Canning simply sat and stared at the unmoving dial, then he pushed open his cab door and dropped down on to the road. He examined the petrol tank and found the answer in thirty seconds. A jagged, finger-sized hole had punctured the tank half-way down and a good fifty per cent of their fuel must have drained away either at the site of the ambush or during the second attack. The hole must have been made either by a broken branch as he crashed the ambulance through the bush, or, more likely, by one of the razor-sharp throwing spears hitting the tank head on.

He stood up slowly and went to the back of the ambulance. Rona already had the door open for him to enter. She said wearily:

'What is it this time?'

Canning studied her, seeing Jenny again in the blue eyes and golden, baby-doll hair. 'Nothing much,' he said. 'One of our black friends was inconsiderate enough to chuck a ruddy great spear into our petrol tank. We're completely out of fuel.'

Silence greeted him, and then Hardman roused himself and said:

'How far are we from Sakinda?'

'About two miles. No more.'

Hardman's pain-ravaged face twisted into a contrived grin. 'It's your unlucky day, Corporal. You're the only man fit enough to walk.'

'I know.' Canning looked around at the pale, sweatstained faces around him. 'I'll make it as fast as I can. I should be able to get back from Sakinda with a lorry in less than an hour. I'll get the two sten guns out of the cab and leave them here in case the Bantu catch up with you before I return. It's unlikely that they're still on our trail, but if they are you'll at least be able to defend yourselves.'

He hurried to the cab and returned a few seconds later with a sten in each

166

hand. He gave Spencer's to Morris, his own he laid beside Delayney.

Rona said, 'Shall I get back on the roof?'

He shook his head, 'There's not much point this time, the surrounding bush is too thick. You won't see them until they come round that last bend in the road, and then you can see them just as easily from the ambulance.'

Rona said, 'I didn't realise — '

'It doesn't matter.' Canning glanced down at Baxter on the floor, 'If I help you sit up and prop some pillows behind you can you cover the back trail?'

Baxter smiled, 'Can do.'

With Rona's help Canning helped the tall man into position, rearranging the pillows that supported his shattered foot and ankle. Baxter's lean face stiffened with pain for a moment and then relaxed. He pulled his sten closer and affirmed that he was both capable and comfortable.

Canning turned to Delayney, 'How about you? Can you still fire a sten if I help you over on to your stomach?'

Delayney grinned, 'As the man says — can do.'

Rona protested sharply, 'That's not necessary. I can fire the sten gun. There's no need to twist him about.'

Canning hesitated for a moment and then Hardman said:

'No disrespects, Ma'am. But the private is a trained soldier and there's nothing wrong with his shoulders and arms: I think he'll make a better job of handling a sten than you could.'

Rona still looked rebellious, but before she could protest any farther Delayney grinned and added:

'You'd better pay attention to Hardman, Ma'am. The big basket always lives up to his name.'

Canning settled the argument by helping Delayney to turn over and face the back of the ambulance. He placed a pillow under the Irishman's chest to raise him up comfortably on his elbows and handed him the sten. Delayney gripped the weapon with both hands and smiled:

'Thanks, Corp.'

Canning acknowledged the smile and then turned back to Rona. 'If you watch through the communication panel you'll be able to keep an eye on the road ahead,' he told her. 'If you really want to handle a sten and the need arises you'd better borrow one from our ginger-headed friend. He'll probably have a bit of difficulty firing with one arm.'

Morris looked hurt. 'I'm all right, Corp. Honest I am.'

Canning grinned, 'Argue it out between you.'

Hardman raised his head from the pillow and said weakly, 'There's no argument, Corporal. You'll take Private Morris's sten gun.'

Canning looked startled, 'If the stens are needed at all they'll be needed here. The Bantu are on the trail behind us.'

'You'll take one sten gun,' Hardman ordered weakly. 'If you fail to reach Sakinda then the rest of us are as good as finished. And one unarmed white man would make too tempting a target for any stray warriors who might cross your path.'

Canning saw the sense in the big Sergeant's words. Morris held the sten gun towards him and he accepted it without any further dissent. Hardman's head and shoulders sagged back on his bed.

Canning found his gaze meeting Rona's worried eyes, and he knew that she was far more troubled than any of the men. Apart from the indomitable Baxter they had all been unconscious through much of the carnage and bloodshed that she had been forced to witness, and he realised suddenly that apart from her one outbreak of hysteria she had showed up remarkably well. She was a woman, after all, and most of them would have broken completely under the terrible strain. He thought abruptly that Jenny would have been reduced to a gibbering idiot, and subconsciously he separated the army nurse and his ex-fiancée for the first time in his mind.

When he spoke he tried to include a note of re-assurance in his voice, 'I'll be back in less than an hour, Lieutenant. You should be all right until then.'

The change of approach brought response and she smiled faintly. 'Good luck, Corporal.'

The words brought back a mind picture of Holland at the stream and caused exactly the opposite effect to that intended. He said quietly, 'Don't say that, Lieutenant. To me it's — it's like tempting fate.' He gave her another brief smile to rob the words of any offence, for he had offended her far too much already.

She made no answer and he turned and stepped down from the back of the ambulance. He hesitated for a moment, but then felt certain that if there was anything that he might have forgotten then Hardman would think of it. He raised his sten gun in a parting salute and then circled round the ambulance to walk the last two miles into Sakinda.

After a hundred yards the ambulance was lost to view behind a bend in the road and from then onwards Canning walked with a sense of complete loneliness. There was nothing but the dusty uneven surface stretching interminably ahead, and the

171

flanking barriers of thorn and bush on either side. Fortunately the bush here was high and dense, and as the sun was now on the last downward slope of the sky he was able to keep in the shade close to the right-hand barrier. He moved briskly at a good marching pace with his sten held loosely at the ready across his stomach, wondering morosely why the hell anyone should want to fight over this desolate part of Africa anyway.

He made good time for the first mile and then his pace began to falter. His feet felt as though they were encased in twin heat-sealed ovens and his legs seemed as though the bones had been replaced by a not very solid form of jelly. The heat was wearing like a heavy rasp at his fading strength and he could think of nothing nearer to ecstasy than the opportunity to pull off his boots and throw them away. He plodded on doggedly for another half-mile, and then he saw the smoke.

The sight brought him to an abrupt halt, his grip tightening automatically on the sten. For the last few hundred yards the surrounding bush had been dwindling in density and now he could see a long distance ahead. A quarter of a mile away he could see the tops of the forest giants that formed the first ramparts of the thickening jungle behind Sakinda rising above the level of the bush and scrubland. And drifting as though balanced on the outstretched branches of the higher trees was an almost stationary pall of thick black smoke. As he watched more dark swirls spiralled upwards, ascending languidly into the still air. An invisible tic began jerking in Canning's stomach, and despite the fact that he was standing in the full sun, the sweat began to cool on the back of his neck.

For one single, self-deluding moment he tried to believe that the lazy smoke coils must come from the cooking fires of the villagers. But then reality forced him to open his mind. He doubted whether a thousand cooking fires could have caused a smoke pall the size of the dark, sinister cloud that now overhung Sakinda. For long moments he stood rigidly in the centre of the road, staring grimly at the ominous scene ahead, and then he continued warily towards the village.

There was no turning back now, for he had to find help, or at the least, petrol to move the stranded ambulance. The wounded men he had left behind could not possibly walk, and regardless of whatever had happened at Sakinda, it was up to him to assess the new situation and do the best he could.

He was fully alert now, his eyes narrowed to search the fartherest reaches of the road, his ears tensed for any warning of impending danger. The weight of tiredness was fading away again and the stubborn streak that was the most dominant part of his nature was coming back to the fore. The sten gun supplied solid, comforting companionship in his hands, and he was thankful for Hardman's insistence that he should not go unarmed.

He kept close to the side of the road, ready to step quickly into the bush at the first sign of any movement on the road ahead. Some of the creeping thorns snagged at his legs as he passed but they were an unnoticed discomfort. Even the killing heat of the sun was forgotten now.

His steps became slower as he drew nearer to the smoke cloud, and his mouth began to dry up all over again. The bush was becoming denser, thickening towards the jungle wall behind the village. Several hundred yards ahead the road vanished behind a bend, and a hundred yards beyond that curve in the trail was the compound of Sakinda. The smoke pall was becoming blacker, uglier, and more threatening with every moment.

Canning approached the bend with the utmost care, and then inched his way slowly around it. The road was still not straight enough for him to see directly into the compound and he left it in order to move closer through the bush. He was half crouching now, using one hand to gently clear the branches away from his face. A twig snapped loudly beneath his descending foot and the sound travelled through his body in a vibrant shudder and jammed in his throat. He swallowed hard, tightening his sweating grip about his sten and gingerly pushed on.

He could smell the smoke now, and felt its acrid sting burning in his lungs. The bush seemed uncannily silent, but from the village came the sound of jabbering voices, mirthless laughter, and the sudden, nerve-chilling throb of native drums.

The village seemed much farther from that bend in the road than Canning remembered, and every moment he expected to come out in full view of the tiny scattering of mud huts around the dusty compound, but every gap in the bush revealed nothing but more bush, more branches and more thorns. Canning's nerves became a tangle of raw ends, each one jumping violently as the cold touch of fear passed over them.

The noise from the village was louder now, swelling to the pulsing, rising beat of the drums. Primitive savagery throbbed in every note, and the only change between now and the Africa a thousand years ago lay in the fact that the black warriors of the Congo were no longer armed simply with the spears and bows of their ancestors, but were fully supplied with deadly modern rifles from the armouries of Katanga.

Abruptly the bush ended, and Canning found himself facing a closely woven barrier of shoulder-high bamboo. He recalled from memory that there had been a bamboo grove behind some of the huts on the south side of the compound, and he knew that Sakinda was directly beyond the inpenetratable, feathery-topped barrier.

He circled the bamboos slowly, moving with infinite care and finally sinking flat to worm the last few yards on his stomach. The bamboos ended and he crawled up to a cluster of wait-a-bit thorn on the edge of the village and peered cautiously between the spiky branches.

The compound was full of Bantu warriors, their black bodies glistening and whirling as they abandoned themselves to the driving rhythm of the drums, their faces contorted and every limb twitching in spasms of ecstasy to the ritual movements of the dance. Many of them were already drunk or else trapped in the trance-like grip of the music.

Canning's gaze moved slowly around the village and he saw that not one of the pathetic mud and wattle huts remained. Instead there was nothing but a series of burnt out shells, blackened circles of fallen timbers, their charred ends still exuding whisps of dying smoke. He wondered what had happened to Sergeant Riley and the other men who had been left behind with the supplies, and then suddenly he knew.

On the far side of the compound stood three great gnarled trees, and with a nauseating surge of horror Canning realised that a white corpse dangled head downwards from every branch. But they were not white corpses — they were red. Every body had been stripped and mutilated with unbelievable bestiality.

The Bantu were celebrating their victory, and Canning was watching the aftermath of murder.

The Listener in the Maize

It was all too plain what had happened.
The Bantu had massacred Holland's
detachment at the stream, and then,
flushed with their success, they had
taken the direct forest paths through
the jungle and bush to attack Sakinda
while the ambulance had been following
the long, slow curve of the road. Sergeant
Riley and his men had most probably
been scattered about the village, relaxing
and unsuspecting as the black warriors
wriggled closer through the bush and the
cultivated patches of maize and potatoes.
They must have been butchered with
hardly any resistance.

Canning looked again at the blood-
soaked corpses dangling on the far side
of the compound and felt his stomach
heaving with violent spasms of sickness.
He bit his teeth hard together, closing
his eyes and burying his face in the grass
beneath him until the nausea had passed.

Then he forced himself to look again.

It was impossible to distinguish the identity of any of the murdered men, for they had been mutilated beyond recognition. The drums were growing louder now, an evil, frightening sound that was only matched by the grotesque contortions of the dancers. There must have been at least two hundred tribesmen filling the compound, naked but for their loin cloths and an occasional blood-stained army jacket or a blue beret. The remains of the huts still smouldered, and the forbidding smoke pall now hovered directly overhead.

Canning closed his eyes again to shut out the barbaric scene and forced himself to think. He realised that if he had been driving the ambulance instead of approaching on foot he would have driven straight into Sakinda before the warning note of the drums had started, and by now he and his companions would be decorating one of those three tall trees beside Riley and his men. The thought was like an injection of ice into his bowels and he offered a silent prayer of thanks to the unknown Katangan who had punctured his petrol tank, even though it now faced him with the seemingly impossible problem of obtaining more petrol.

He was grimly aware that time was vital, for the smaller party of tribesmen who had tried to head him off on the road — most probably to prevent him getting a warning through to Riley — would by now be hurrying back to Sakinda. The odds were that they would again ignore the road and cut through the quicker jungle paths which they would know so well, but even if they missed the ambulance completely they would still report its escape to their leaders once they reached the village. Every minute that the ambulance remained stranded on the Sakinda-Kasuvu road placed its occupants in terrible danger.

Slowly Canning raised his head and opened his eyes. He didn't know where to head for once he got the ambulance moving, but the one fact that was starkly clear was that it had to be moved. And to move it he had to have petrol.

His eyes ranged once more around the compound. He had missed the two heavy army lorries that had been left behind, but now he saw that they too were mere gutted shells, half obscured by the leaping bodies of the Congo tribesmen. The stack of petrol cans and supplies that had been left behind had been covered with a heavy tarpaulin beneath the very trees that now supported the bodies of the men left to guard them, but Canning was unable to distinguish whether or not they were still there.

He swore softly as he attempted to peer through the distant, jostling legs of the dancers, but still he could see nothing beyond. He backed away from his sheltering cluster of thorns, moving with utmost care until he was back in the denser safety of the bush, and then he began to circle round the village.

His progress was painfully slow, a combination of crouching, crawling, and in places slithering on his stomach. His heart thumped heavily in his chest and the sten gun in his hand was more of a liability than anything else as it

182

snagged repeatedly in the undergrowth. The bush consisted of nothing but wait-a-bit thorn, bristling with dagger-sharp barbs that stabbed at his shrinking flesh. The crescendo of the drums and the whoops of the Bantu played torment with his nerves with every step he made.

He circled half-way round the village and then moved closer once more. A patch of waist-high nettles barred his way, but instinct warned him that their sting would be far more virulent than the English hedgerow variety and he bypassed them warily. The bush thinned out again and the smoking shell of one of the burned-out huts came into view. Canning dropped low on his stomach and inched forward as cautiously as possible.

He could again see into the village, but still the whirling dancers blocked his line of vision and he could not quite see whether the petrol and supplies were untouched. His heart quickened in tune with the drums and his stomach trembled as he realised that he would have to go closer.

Directly below him were several

cultivated plots of knee-high maize that reached almost to the back of the nearest burned-out huts. The few sloping yards that separated him from his dubious shelter consisted of long grass and stunted shrubs. Canning wondered if he should leave his sten gun behind, for it was an encumberance, and would prove practically useless in the face of the odds against him if the Bantu should become aware of his presence. He hesitated, but the sten was too comforting a friend to leave behind and he finally took it with him.

He slithered swiftly through the long yellow grass, practically falling into the concealing safety of the patch of maize. He lay full length beneath the thick stalks with their half-ripened corn cobs, regaining his breath and waiting for his heart to stop its insane pounding. Then he raised his head for a slow look round.

Nothing had changed. The huts still smoked and the Bantu still abandoned themselves to the hypnotic fascination of the drums. Canning turned his head a little farther and saw that at least one of the huts on this side of the village was still standing, its thatched roof was badly charred, but somehow it had been spared total destruction. It was one of the largest huts that the village had possessed, and he believed that it had belonged to the headman.

Grimly Canning began to wriggle closer over the soft, hoed earth beneath the maize stalks. His course was taking him gradually closer to the solitary hut, but that was chance and not intention, for he was merely attempting to reach a better vantage point. He reached the very edge of the maize patch, less than a yard from the smouldering circle of ashes that marked the site of the hut that had stood next door to the one remaining. He raised his head and shoulders slightly for a long, careful look, and then felt a completely undefinable swell of emotion within him.

The stacked cans of petrol were still there under the tarpaulin, but the emotion was undefinable because he still had to find some method of getting them away.

He didn't know whether he was relieved or not.

Having established that the cans were there there was nothing else that he could do from his present position and he began to retreat slowly through the maize plot. Then, quite abruptly, and quite clearly, he heard a sound that stopped him dead in his tracks. It was the sound of a voice coming from the solitary hut only a few yards away, and the words were unmistakably uttered in English.

Canning froze stiffly into the soft earth, straining his eyes through the narrow gaps between the thick-leaved stalks of maize, and then he saw that two men had stepped from the hut and now stood facing each other in its shadow. The man fartherest away was Congolese, an old negro who appeared to be a chief of some kind. But the man with his back towards Canning was a white man.

Canning realised that the stranger could only be one of Katanga's white mercenaries, and probably the man whom Holland had been ordered to find. He stared at the tall, darkly-bronzed figure and suddenly knew that this must be the man who had planned the massacre at the stream, and then led the Bantu on to slaughter the unfortunates now hanging above the compound. He stared, and a terrible, murderous rage took slow and absolute control of his limbs, and without any conscious effort the sten gun moved silently in his hands. It was as if the sten possessed a life of its own; one moment it was still beneath Canning's outstretched fingers, and the next it had inexorably straightened, the snout thrusting through the maize leaves and levelling squarely on the mercenary's broad back. Canning's knuckle whitened on the trigger and Larocque was within a hairsbreadth of savage, avenging death.

Sanity stepped in. Sanity that screamed desperately that if Larocque died now then Canning must surely die also, speared by the blood hungry horde still stamping in the ritual of the dance not forty yards away. The ambulance would be discovered and the wounded men cut to pieces. And Rona Waring would suffer worse, for she would most certainly be raped before she was killed.

Canning knew that he could not kill Larocque.

The sten sank slowly down to the earth and Canning lay trembling at the horror of what he had almost done. The mercenary and the old negro continued to argue beside the hut.

Larocque's command of the Bantu language was fairly good providing he spoke slowly, but now anger had over-ruled his patience and he had resorted to English which Mambiro understood perfectly well.

'There is no time for feasting and dancing,' he was saying furiously. 'There is still the ambulance that escaped with several of the white soldiers aboard. The dancing can begin after we have taken that.'

Mambiro shrugged, 'The dance has already begun.'

'Then stop it!' Larocque's voice was harsh and commanding. 'You are their chief. Stop the dancing and give me a dozen of your best hunters to help me find the ambulance.'

Mambiro's expression became ugly. 'I have already sent one party of my hunters to catch up with this — this ambulance. They will stop it for you.'

'But I must be sure.' Larocque controlled himself with an effort, 'The man I want was not among the dead at the stream, neither was he here at Sakinda — and that means that he must be aboard that ambulance. I know that he was with this troop of soldiers, and I am almost certain that I saw him during the ambush at the stream. He *must* be aboard that ambulance!'

Mambiro said angrily, 'The warriors I have sent are enough. They will have stopped your ambulance by now. There is no need to send more.'

'By this time your warriors should have caught us up. Perhaps they have failed and are afraid to face your anger.'

'The jungle will kill the white man anyway. It does not matter.'

'But this white man I want alive. I must make him talk.' Larocque's control was slipping and his voice was rising to a shout.

Mambiro gave him a hard look. 'Why is this one white man so important?'

'That is my business. You promised that he would be taken alive so that I could talk with him.'

Mambiro suddenly smiled but the smile was without humour. 'As you say white friend — the man in the ambulance is your business. But it is no concern of mine. My concern is the freedom of Katanga and Katanga must come before your personal quarrels. We needed you to lead us into battle against the white soldiers but next time the white soldiers may not be so many and we shall not need you at all. Consider well before you quarrel with me.'

Canning was listening intently now and he saw the mercenary's tall frame stiffen with suppressed fury:

'Perhaps you are right Mambiro.' His voice was hard and brittle. 'But the white soldiers are not fools. They are more likely to come in greater numbers — not less — and then you will need me again.

And perhaps then I will refuse.'

'And perhaps — ' Mambiro smiled again, ' — perhaps we will kill you. Think well, Bwana Larocque.'

There was a scornful warning behind the word Bwana, and without waiting for an answer the old negro turned away and walked towards the dancers in the compound. Larocque stood with his fists clenched tightly by his sides and his dark face thunderous with fury. Then he spun on his heel and vanished inside the hut.

Canning's mind was already revolving unsteadily with the stunning implications of what he had just heard, but he knew that there was no time to think the matter over now. The ambulance was in far greater danger than he had ever realised and he had to get back. He began to wriggle swiftly backwards through the maize patch until the covering stalks came to an end. Again he faced the few yards of open grassland between the cultivated plots and the edge of the bush, but the sun was at last on the final decline and long shadows fell across the intervening space. He made sure that the blacks were still lost in the rituals of the dance and then thrust himself across the danger stretch in a fast crawling rush. He collapsed behind the nearer bushes and lay there breathing heavily. His movements had attracted no attention and after a few moments he gratefully began to put more distance between himself and the village.

It took him ten minutes to regain the road and then he began to run as fast as he could away from Sakinda. It was still imperative that he obtained enough petrol to get the ambulance to safety, but before he could hope to reach the stacked cans in the compound he would have to break up the dancing and draw the blacks away. He had already thought of a plan to provide the necessary diversion, but he could not possibly carry it out on his own; either Morris or Rona Waring had to help him.

The sun had died to a red half-disc on the western skyline and very soon it had dropped completely out of sight. Dusk was swift and fleeting and by the time he neared the ambulance the moon had appeared to relieve the tropic night. The ambulance loomed out of the shadows like some great, square, primeval beast from the dimmer realms of Africa's past; an armoured monster with sinister moonlight flecking its steel sides.

He shouted out to identify himself as he came to a panting stop, for in the semi-darkness either Rona or Morris might have shot him by mistake through the communication panel and the empty windscreen. There was an answering shout from Rona and then he circled round the stationary vehicle to reach the back doors. Baxter and Delayney slowly lowered their sten guns as he approached, and Rona came forward to help him climb in.

She said unsteadily, 'What — what's happened? We heard the drums.'

Canning leaned against Garner's bed, his chest still heaving. He said grimly, 'So did I. I almost walked into the village before they started up. Sakinda is full of the same warriors who attacked the convoy at the stream.'

'But that's impossible.' Rona's voice was horrified.

Canning shook his head, 'I'm afraid it isn't impossible. They cut directly across country. It's much quicker than following the road. Besides, that mud hole delayed us for quite a while.' He looked slowly around the shadowed faces in the darkness, too breathless to talk any more. Rona was staring at him with sick despair. Baxter's lean face was indescribably grim. Delayney's face was hidden by the darker patch of shadow from the bed above him, but Morris's expression was exactly as Canning imagined his own must have been when he first saw the bodies in the compound.

Then Hardman stirred, raising himself painfully on to his elbows. He stared at Canning and said harshly:

'What happened to the men? Sergeant Riley and the men who were left behind — what happened to them?'

Canning swallowed hard, 'They're dead. All of them.'

He wouldn't elaborate any farther than that, but it was enough. Hardman's massive, squared face seemed to shrink beneath the grey-white skin and his eyes closed with a deeper, more lasting agony than physical pain could ever bring. Canning watched the great shoulders sink back on the bed and realised that Hardman was much, much more than the illiterate bull he had first supposed. The big Sergeant could feel the death thrust of every single man who had been under his command. They only died once, but Hardman died inside, again and again, with every one of them.

There was a moment's silence, and Delayney said savagely:

'Why? Why should the bastards want to murder us all? We're only supposed to be in this blasted country to help them.'

Canning remembered the conversation he had overheard from the maize patch, and his stomach grew cold as he stared into the darkness at the Irishman's face.

'I don't know,' he said, and his voice was filled with uncontrollable menace. 'But somebody here does. There's a white mercenary leading the Bantu, and he's only leading them because he needs them to help him catch up with somebody aboard this ambulance.'

There was a moment of shocked, disbelieving silence. Canning stared at each face in turn but only Rona's face registered with any clarity. She looked helplessly frightened and confused. Then Baxter's granite face cracked and he demanded slowly:

'What are you trying to say, Corp?'

Canning recounted the conversation he had overheard. He finished by saying grimly, 'I heard the mercenary addressed as Larocque. Does that name mean anything to anybody?'

No one answered. Canning said sharply:
'Morris?'

The little man started abruptly, his eyes popping in astonishment beneath the bloodstained bandage that encircled his temple.

'No. No, Corp,' he blurted, 'it doesn't mean anything to me.'

Canning looked at the tall man propped up at his feet:
'Baxter?'

Baxter gave a slow, negative shake of his head.

'Delayney?'

Delayney's face was still invisible in the darkness. He said belligerently, 'No, Corp. Not me.'

Canning glanced at Hardman. The Sergeant was unmoving, his eyes still closed, but without knowing why Canning was suddenly certain that it could not be Hardman. At least, not knowingly.

Slowly his gaze turned to the top bed. To Garner, the sick patient who was only a name; a feverish body with no personality who could be anything.

He said to Rona, 'How is he?'

She said uncertainly, 'I think the worst of the fever's broken. He's been quiet ever since you left.'

Canning said harshly, 'He's been quiet all the time. A convenient way to get out of all the fighting and dying that's been going on.'

Rona suddenly forgot her fear and confusion and sprang with unexpected violence to Garner's defence. 'That man is too sick to have known anything of what's been going on,' she blazed furiously. 'Do you think I don't know enough about my own job to know whether a man is genuinely ill or not.'

Canning felt his own temper subside and knew that the outburst had been well deserved. Garner's fever was far too violent to be any form of pretence. He said clumsily:

'I'm sorry, Lieutenant. I wasn't thinking straight.'

She simmered down at his apology, but before anything else could be said Hardman was again raising himself slowly from his pillow. He had to struggle to hold his head up and he seemed completely unaware of what had passed since he had last spoken.

'Corporal.' His voice was weak but steady, 'What about the petrol? Is there any way of getting enough to drive the ambulance clear?'

Canning realised that the Sergeant's mind was still following the most important track. Any argument between themselves could be settled later, right now he had to think about obtaining the petrol to get them out of their present position.

He said quietly, 'The petrol cans are still stacked in the compound where we left them, but as the village is full of Larocque's tribesmen I'll need a diversion of some kind to help me get it.' He glanced at Rona and Morris who stood side by side at the back of the ambulance, and finished. 'One of you will have to help me.'

Morris shuffled uneasily, and then Rona said in a very clear voice:

'Then you'd better tell me what to do.'

Canning hesitated. She was a woman and already she had suffered one outburst of hysterics, and she might easily lose her nerve and let him down. But on the other hand Morris was badly weakened and handicapped by his head wound and his broken arm, and could just as easily collapse if he was allowed to wander around in the bush. He looked from one to the other, and then found that he couldn't avoid Rona's eyes. There was nothing babyish in their blue depths any more, and although fear was still there there was determination as well, an inner strength that he had never seen in Jenny's eyes.

Suddenly, savagely, he told himself that he was not dealing with Jenny any longer. He was dealing with Rona Waring. In appearance they were identical, but underneath they were worlds apart. Rona had broken once, but was there any woman who would not have done the same? He owed her another chance.

He said quietly, 'All right, Lieutenant, this is what I want you to do.'

The Night of Fire

Canning and Rona hurried in concentrated silence along the darkened road to Sakinda. The moon was rising and its pale, shadowed light marked their path with faint luminosity. The surrounding jungle and bush was strangely alive with distant, surreptitious rustlings of sound; the croaking of a frog and the gentle whisper of ghost fingers stirring the branches; the hoarse, coughing bark of a far away hyena; and all the other unexplained suggestions of movement that made up the unseen backcloth of the African night.

Canning still carried his sten but now he was also armed with the evil-looking knife that Morris had picked up after the struggle with the lone warrior who had leaped into the back of the ambulance during the last attack. Rona had Baxter's cigarette lighter buttoned securely in the breast pocket of her blouse.

They moved at a fast pace because Canning was badly worried. He knew that for the moment there was not much danger of the main party of the Bantu being distracted from the festivities at Sakinda, but the smaller party who had been detailed to head him off on the road was another matter entirely. By now the smaller party had had plenty of time to catch up with the ambulance, or, if they had taken the forest paths, to reach Sakinda, and their whereabouts was Canning's chief concern. He knew from the conversation he had overheard that the tribesmen had good reason to fear the combined wrath of Larocque and Mambiro if they returned to report failure, and he was terribly afraid that even now they could be creeping up to launch a second attack on the immobilised ambulance. It was true that the men in the ambulance knew the facts and were fully prepared, but they had very little ammunition left for the sten guns, and held fixed to their beds by their wounds their resistance would be sorely limited.

The only sounds were those of the night and the scuff of their feet through the dust of the road. There was neither time nor inclination for idle conversation and they both knew exactly what they had to do. The night was cool after the gruelling heat of the day, but their minds were too occupied to take notice of the slight chill. The muffled throb of the drums still carried clearly through the still air as the triumphant Katangans celebrated their victory.

When they were still half-a-mile from the village Canning took Rona by the arm and turned right into the bush. He simply gestured the way with his sten and she allowed him to guide her without protest. The grass was knee-deep as they picked their way between islands of thicket and tumbles of sandstone rock, and Rona flinched as the long, matted tangles wrapped around her legs. Canning wondered whether she was thinking the same disturbing thoughts that had suddenly become uppermost in his own mind, and then decided that she wasn't. The African bush possessed an extensive variety of highly venomous snakes, and if she too had visions of a coiled cobra or mamba he doubted whether she could have concealed them so completely.

They pushed on as fast as the restraining grassland would allow until finally they came out on the savannah plain on the north side of Sakinda. The village was now immediately on their left with the rising barrier of jungle behind it, and from here the rolling grassland swept right up to the cultivated fields and the cattle kraals on the outskirts of the fire-ravaged huts. The plain could have been mistaken from a distance for a field of waving wheat, unbroken except for an isolated knuckle of red rock. It was tinder-dry, and the wind was still blowing from the north-west.

Canning said quietly, 'This is it, Lieutenant. Give me fifteen minutes to get to the edge of the village and then get busy with your cigarette lighter. Make sure that the grass is well alight and the wind will do the rest. As soon as you've finished double back to the ambulance as fast as you can. Forget about me. Can you do that?'

Rona fumbled in her breast pocket for her cigarette lighter. 'I can do it,' she said, 'you can trust me.'

Her voice was not quite as definite as her words, and she trembled slightly as the sound of the drums rolled across the dark, silent plain. But Canning had a strange, inexplicable faith in her ability. He handed her his sten gun and said:

'You'd better take this — just in case anything goes wrong.'

She accepted the gun reluctantly, her blue eyes searching his face. 'Are you sure you won't be in more need of it?'

Canning smiled. 'If I'm spotted I doubt whether an antitank gun would be of much use to me. And besides, it's a bloody nuisance when you're crawling about on hands and knees.'

For a moment they faced each other, groping for something to say.

Then Rona said, 'The last time I tried to wish you luck you stopped me. But be careful, Corporal. If it doesn't work out, don't take any suicide risks.'

Her voice was level, and completely without emotion, and for a moment he wondered whether she was more worried about the helpless men in the ambulance, or the fact that the Bantu might rob her of the opportunity to watch his court martial. In the same moment he knew that the thought was unjust, viciously unjust, and he felt almost as guilty as if he had uttered it aloud.

He said, 'I'll be careful. Give me fifteen minutes.' And then he turned away and left her, hurrying swiftly through the dark sea of savannah towards the sounds of revelry that came from the village.

Rona watched him go, fading away into the African night. She shivered at the sound of the drums and felt fear crawling between her shoulder blades. She felt utterly alone in a hostile world and even the sten in her hands provided no comfort to the frightening torrent of her thoughts. She had to make a conscious physical effort to look down at the watch on her wrist, and she wondered how many lifetimes would pass before the next fifteen minutes came to an end.

Canning had already left the savannah plain, veering left to regain the cover of the bush. The moon had passed behind a bank of cloud and he stumbled blindly forwards through the darkness, crushing down curse after curse as the thorns and branches stabbed at him with unseen arms. Once an owl hooted at him from the higher tangles of a thicket and his heart almost kicked through his ribs. He pulled the knife from his belt and slashed as silently as possible at the spiky talons of thorn that snagged in his clothes.

As he neared the outskirts of the village his pace slowed and he covered the last fifty yards with the utmost care. The frenzied chanting of the Bantu and the pulse of the drums now filled the whole of the night and the rustlings of the jungle were drowned into insignificance. Then from the bushes just ahead of him came an abrupt, high-pitched feminine giggle.

Canning froze, his knife poised to hack at a thorny branch that had hooked into the sleeve of his shirt. The giggle came again, a half-sensuous, half-caressing sound, followed by a squirming rustling movement in the long grass. Canning realised that not all of the Bantu were hypnotised by the music and the dance. At least one of the lusty young warriors was regarding the village girls of Sakinda as the spoils of war; and at least one of the dusky belles had resigned to the inevitable and was preparing to enjoy paying the price.

Moving with infinite care Canning disentangled his arm from the thorns and slowly circled the clump of bushes. The giggling continued and he offered a silent prayer of thanks to the negro maiden who was so obviously unashamed to show her appreciation. If she had made love in swooning silence with her eyes closed like an English girl, he thought grimly, he would have blundered straight into them.

He moved well away from the concealing bushes, even more alert now in case he should encounter any similar couples. His heart was racing and the cold breeze chilled the sweat on his face. He knew that he did not have many more minutes before Rona fired the grassland and he turned his course once more towards the village.

The bush began to peter out and he slipped down on his stomach to cover the last few feet, pulling himself into a patch of inky shadow behind some small slabs of worn rock. He was on exactly the opposite side of the village to the spot where he had laid earlier in the evening and he had a clear view of what was happening. Half-a-dozen large cooking fires now blazed around the edges of the compound and the flickering tongues of flame threw a bizarre red glow upon the leaping dancers. The natives squatting over their drums grinned with feverish excitement as the palms of their hands swept in a blur of pulsating movement over the stretched animal hides. There was no sign of either Mambiro or Larocque, but the mutilated corpses still dangled from the tall trees, looking even more hideous than before in the smoky light from the fires.

Canning searched for the petrol and

saw that the stack of cans beneath the tarpaulin had not been moved. Where he lay he was not a hundred feet away from them.

There was nothing he could do now but watch and wait, and pray that no other giggling couples tripped over him while seeking the privacy of the bushes. He could see the sweat glistening on the naked black bodies in the compound and he realised that most of them were already drunk; a fact which suited his purpose admirably. He wanted absolute confusion and chaos in order to succeed with his wild plan, and if the Bantu were incapable with drink then so much the better. He tested the wind to ensure that it was still blowing from the north west and prayed that it wouldn't change.

He had no wrist watch of his own so he could not tell exactly how many minutes had elapsed since he had parted from Rona, but he was sure that the quarter hour must be almost up. He waited for the first signs of the grass fire she was to start and felt his resolve beginning to weaken when nothing happened. He wondered whether she had lost her nerve, or whether the cigarette lighter had failed to function. It had worked perfectly in the ambulance but it might have jammed, or she might have lost it. He should have given her his own to make doubly sure. Perhaps she had been surprised by some wandering natives; but then he would have heard the sound of the sten — if she had been given a chance to use it. Perhaps she had slipped and twisted an ankle or broken a leg — or perhaps she had fallen victim to the lunging attack of a hissing mamba, disturbed from its coiled nesting place in the long grass. Perhaps . . . Perhaps . . . Perhaps . . .

He caught the first faint taste of smoke and felt an infinite sense of relief seep through him It was not the smoke from the fires in the compound, for the wind was wafting those swirls away into the jungle on the far side of the village. This delicate, acrid sting in his nostrils came from behind him, borne on the breeze from the broad savannah plain.

His hand gripped more tightly around the knife, not such a comforting feel as the sten, but better than nothing none the less. His resolve hardened again as he told himself that Rona had done her share and now it was up to him. He hoped that she wouldn't lose herself in the bush as she hurried back to the ambulance.

The smell of smoke was stronger now, much stronger, and he heard the distant spit and crackle of the flames, a hushed sound as yet, but one that must swell into a hungry roar as the fire swept over the rolling plain. He was lying full in its path, but he knew that this was the best position he could have taken up. When the panic came at least he could be sure that none of the blacks would flee in this direction.

He looked back over his shoulder and saw the black smoke clouds furling upwards to his right and behind him. The moonlight was bright again and the ominous, lengthening pall was stark and clear against the star-bright sky. As he watched slender needles of orange flame darted skywards and died again, but each succeeding flicker of fire was stronger and brighter than the one before. The sound was increasing, a sinister crackling as the long yellow grass blades twisted away from the licking heat, only to whither, blackened and charred, beneath the advancing flames. Canning began to cough as the smoke penetrated his throat and lungs, and tears sprang sharply into his eyes. He could feel the first waves of heat rolling over his shoulders.

The Bantu still continued to whirl and stamp in the compound, transfixed by the magnetic influence of the ritual dance and the commanding pounding of the drums. Canning watched them in horrific fascination, willing them to look up, to break and scatter before the advancing wall of fire. He had a sudden terrible fear that he would have to either remain where he was until the flames engulfed him, or else be driven helplessly forwards into the village while the Bantu were still there. Not even the proximity of burning death had the power to break the trance-like spell of the drums that held every warrior fast in its grip.

Then abruptly there came a shriek of

pure terror from behind him, followed by a frenzied upheaval in the bushes. A completely naked young warrior leapt into the open as though the very gates of hell were swinging open at his heels, waving his arms and shouting at the top of his voice as he blundered frantically towards the dancers. Behind him ran a terrified girl, her chocolate body equally nude and showing no signs of maidenly modesty as she bolted after her fleeing lover. Canning remembered the couple he had almost bumped into as he approached the village, and realised that this time they had been wholly interrupted with a vengeance.

The nearer of the dancers stopped, but still the drums beat on. Then slowly realisation sank into the primitive minds and one by one the drums stopped. The more feverish of the dancers whirled on, but slowly they too shuffled to a halt and stared towards the north-west. The sky was full of smoke and fire, and the greedy, crackling voice of the flames.

The transformation was abrupt and terrifying. One moment the chanting warriors in the compound were stiff with shock, staring in startled horror, and the next there was complete and absolute chaos and pandemonium. A bomb exploding in the compound could not have caused such a panic-stricken scattering of black bodies. There were screams from the unfortunates who slipped to be trampled by the milling stampede; screams from the scalding impact of overturned cooking pots; and great rending shrieks of agony from those pushed into the blazing fires as their companions fought to get away. In disorder and confusion the Katangans fled to the forest behind the village.

Canning pushed himself upright, feeling the heat roasting his back. Smoke filled his throat and he choked helplessly, tears streaming down his eyes as he staggered forward. Rona had done a magnificent job and the wave of fire rushing down on Sakinda was far bigger than anything Canning had ever intended.

He trampled over a patch of potato plots as he ran, kicking through the dead ashes and embers of one of the huts as he headed for the compound. The heat behind acted as a spur to drive him on and already he was enveloped in swirling clouds of the thick black smoke. Screams continued to echo through the night, swelled by the yelping of dogs and the terrified bellowing from the cattle kraals that housed Sakinda's pathetically small herd of cows. The compound was already empty but for a few drunken natives too helpless to realise what was happening and the grim, blood-soaked sentinels hanging from the three great trees.

Canning stumbled over a discarded drum and almost sprawled flat on his face as he reached the compound, but recovering his balance he ran on to the stacked petrol cans. He pulled up beside them, sobbing for breath as the smoke he inhaled burned in his throat, and pausing to make a hurried inspection of the village. The Bantu had abandoned it completely, and the single large hut, which he guessed had been taken over by Mambiro and Larocque, appeared to be empty. The white mercenary and the

Bantu chief had fled with the rest.

Canning used his knife to slash at the ropes securing the tarpaulin, hurling the heavy covering back with feverish anxiety. The petrol was in large, four-gallon cans and the heat was so intense that he feared the whole lot might suddenly explode in his face. He thrust his knife into his belt and heaved one of the cans down from the stack, and then instinct flashed him a warning a split second before he heard the clumsy rushing movement behind him.

He dropped the can and wheeled to one side, avoiding an uncertain spear thrust that clanged violently off the stack of drums. A few seconds ago the native wielding the spear had been lying in a drunken stupor on the edge of the compound, and he seemed still unaware of the fiery danger sweeping down from the north-west. The urgency of movement around him had gradually penetrated his barely-conscious mind, and he had dimly seen the white man standing by the petrol cans. Had he been sober Canning would have been dead, but having made his one

217

lunge he could only sway drunkenly as he struggled to regain his balance.

Canning had neither time nor conscience. He kicked the reeling warrior savagely in the lower stomach and then booted him again in the face as he went down. The heavy army boot was far more effective than a fist and the negro hit the dusty earth like a falling sack, his spear slithering out of his hand.

Canning turned back to the task in hand and lifted down three more cans of petrol. Two of the four-gallon cans should have been enough for any man to carry, but the mileage consumption of the ambulance was high and Canning determined to return with four. He stood two cans upright, and then balanced the remaining two cans edge on top of them. Standing between the two pairs he wrapped his arms about the top cans and then wriggled his fingers into a firm hand grip on the handles of those standing on the ground. He straightened up, staggering beneath the weight, and then headed for the opening in the bush that marked the Kasuvu road.

The scorching heat hit him full in the face and smoke all but blinded him. Through streaming eyes he saw that the wall of flame had reached the edge of the village and already one or two of the maize plots were crackling as they burned. There was not a negro in sight apart from those too drunk to move. The cattle had broken out of the flimsy kraal and stampeded and he could still hear the frantic bellowing from the direction of the jungle.

He crossed the compound and plunged into the bush along the now-familiar dusty road, moving parallel to the line of fire that had stopped at the edge of the village where there was no more grass and brush on which it could feed. The leaping flames were curving forward over thc village, bowed forwards by the wind as though hungrily searching for more fuel. Already Canning was soaked in sweat, choking and blinded as he struggled on under the killing weight of the four cans. He did not expect to get them all the way back to the ambulance, but if he could only get them well clear of Sakinda he could carry on with one can and then drive back for the remainder.

Canning covered a hundred stumbling yards, refusing to rest until he had turned the bend that hid Sakinda from view. He stopped then, panting for breath, and then slowly he realised that although he should have been moving out of range of the fire he was still wrapped in the swirling smoke, and the flames were still dangerously close behind him.

That was when he realised that the wind had changed. Instead of blowing from the north-west it was now blowing from due north. And the fire, hopelessly out of control, was now sweeping down the left hand side of the road, and threatening to overtake him long before he could rejoin the stranded ambulance.

Race Against the Flames

Canning felt as though an iron fist had fastened a squeezing grip around his labouring heart. The strength drained from his limbs and he was incapable of either thought or movement, incapable of anything except feeling the sick, crushing weight of despair that swamped over him. The towering flames rose fifteen feet into the air, a swirling holocaust of red, yellow and orange, raging beneath the black blanket of twisting smoke. The sound of their approach obliterated everything else and it seemed as though the whole of Africa must be blazing in one hideous night of fire.

For long seconds Canning stared with tear-filled, unbelieving eyes, and then the deep stubborn streak that had been his strongest ally came to his aid once more, forcing down the surge of despair and causing him to turn and hurry on with the precious cans of petrol.

The impossible, punishing weight dragged at his arms until his shoulder muscles screamed with the pain. His lungs were expanded to the limit with each tearing gulp of blistering air, and his arched back-bone felt as though it must surely break and splinter into a thousand pieces. He made another seventy yards with the dust pulling at his feet and the sweat streaming down his face, and then he staggered to another stop, bitterly facing the fact that the Herculean task was beyond him.

He straightened his aching shoulders and relinquished two of the heavy cans, and then with one can in each hand he ran on. After fifty yards he stumbled in a pot-hole and sprawled forwards on his face. What little breath he had was driven from his tortured lungs and he lay there gasping for breath, feeling as though every muscle in his body had been passed through a giant wringer.

But necessity was a cruel spur and after a moment he pushed himself doggedly away from the ground, pausing on his hands and knees to look back at the advancing flames. The fire had spread to the bush on both sides of the road and the army of fiery tongues was marching stolidly towards him at almost regulation walking pace. The wind had dropped slightly and they had not yet overtaken the two cans he had left behind.

Defiance burned in Canning's heart. The wind was fickle and might yet drop more or else change again, and as long as he could keep ahead of the flames there was a slim chance that he could still save all four of the vital cans of petrol. The eight gallons in the two cans beside him should last easily over the hundred miles back to Kasuvu, but with the possibility that the unaccounted part of Larocque's Bantu were still lurking on the Kasuvu road he might be forced to take a different route, and there was no way of knowing how many times he might be forced to change direction. He needed all the petrol he could get. And there was no other possible source of supply if he should abandon any of his hard won prize to the flames. He clenched his teeth with stubborn determination, thrust himself to his feet, and ran swiftly back towards the roaring furnace of blazing bush.

The murderous heat scorched his face as he reached the two cans that still stood upright in the middle of the road. He picked them up as the smoke blinded him once again and then turned to stumble away. The inner lining of his lungs felt as though it had been scraped raw and every hot straining breath was pure agony. Two at a time he moved his precious petrol cans along the endless road, staggering backwards and forwards in a blindly stubborn effort to keep ahead of the flames. He was no longer capable of logical thought and sanity could no longer reach his fuddled mind. He was drugged by the effects of smoke and fire, the terrible aching of his body, and the sole, driving need to save the invaluable cans that threatened to drag his arms clear away from their sockets.

Gradually the distance he ran with each haul became smaller until soon he was barely making a dozen yards at a time. But he was keeping ahead of the pursuing flames and that was enough.

He was thrashing his tiring body to the limits of endurance, toiling in an almost complete mental blackout. Every energy was contributed to the demands of physical exertion and his mind was just a dull, pain-filled blank.

He had passed the point where sanity should have caused him to give up the unequal struggle and leave two of the heavy cans behind, and then suddenly a running figure blundered unexpectedly out of the smoke ahead of him. For a moment he was still blind and he dropped his burden in a clumsy effort to defend himself as they collided heavily in the darkness, and then through streaming eyes he recognised Rona Waring.

For a moment they could only support each other with drunken helplessness, both speechless from the strain of their exertions. Rona's blonde hair was thick with smudges and smuts and her face glistened redly with tears. Her eyes were rimmed with deep, blood-red circles and her lips were parted as she sucked in great gulps of air. Her blouse had burst open again and the flesh beneath was flushed by the light of the flames and slippery with sweat, her breasts straining wildly against the black lace bra. The sten was slung across her shoulders.

Canning found his voice and grated harshly, 'I told you to get straight back to the ambulance.' The words seemed to tear their way out of his throat and he had to shout to make himself heard above the snarl of the fire.

Rona stared into his face, tried to answer and broke into a spasm of coughing. Finally she straightened her face again and said weakly, 'I realised that the wind had changed. I thought — I thought you might need help.'

Canning realised the madness of any argument and pushed his two cans into her hands.

'Take these and get going. I'll catch you up.'

He didn't wait to see whether she obeyed but turned back towards the fire to retrieve the remaining two cans. He lifted them and turned again, and then saw that Rona was obediently struggling back the way she had come with the two four-gallon cans dragging at her sides. He felt the heat searing his back and shoulders and hurried after her as she was swallowed up by the smoke-filled darkness.

Canning had already covered half a mile, but they still had a mile and a half to go before they would reach the waiting ambulance. He knew that even with their combined efforts they would never carry all sixteen gallons of petrol all the way, but he still hoped to get clear of the fire so that he could push on with one can and then drive back for the rest.

Rona toiled magnificently by his side, for although she was breathless from forcing her way in a wide circle through the bush she still had untapped reservoirs of strength. Her eyes were smarting painfully from the biting sting of the smoke and she was coughing badly, but her feet were sure and her legs never faltered. Canning should have been on the point of exhaustion, but new hope and stubborn determination kept him going.

Slowly they began to pull ahead of the

burning bush. The wind had mercifully dropped to the lightest of breezes and only the fire's own momentum propelled it forwards. The night was still festooned in smoke and the skyline behind them was still pierced by dancing spears of red and orange, but at last the grilling heat was no longer flaying their backs. Canning was tempted to ease up and call a rest, but he knew how quickly the wind could build up again behind them and he slogged wearily on. He knew that if the wind should gain any real strength then the fire could sweep down on them like a tidal wave of tumbling flame, and they would be lucky if they had time to abandon the cans and escape with their lives.

From time to time he glanced at Rona stumbling heroically beside him and marvelled at her stamina, the two petrol cans were a man-sized burden and must have been bruising her badly as they battered against her calves and thighs, yet she made no complaint. Her shoulders were bowed beneath the weight and must have been aching as furiously as his own.

For another quarter of a mile they staggered on and then inevitably Rona's strength began to fade. Her shoulders sagged lower and the two cans she carried began to drag in the dust. Canning himself felt more dead than alive with fatigue and when he saw that they had now pulled well ahead of the flames he knew that he had to call a halt.

They lowered the four large cans and stood facing each other in the road, their chests heaving uncontrollably as they drank down luxurious gulps of clean air. They were clear of the smoke clouds now and it was a merciful blessing to be able to draw a breath that did not blister their throats and lungs. The moonlight was bright again now that the sky was no longer blotted from view. The sound of the fire was muffled and less immediate, and the louder rustlings of bush and jungle made themselves heard again.

Canning knew the danger of fatigue taking complete control if they spared themselves for too long, and after a few minutes respite to bring their breathing a little nearer to normal he said weakly:

'We'd better move on — we've got a long way to go.'

Rona looked into his face, still fighting to find the necessary breath to speak.

'Wait,' she blurted at last. 'Wait a minute.' There was a flicker of hope in her painfully bloodshot eyes, and when she took down enough breath to finish there was almost a prayer in her voice. She said, 'I think — I think the wind has changed.'

Canning stared at her, suddenly afraid to believe that it might be true. And then he raised his head to look down the road behind him and felt the strengthening breeze blow cool on the singed flesh of his face. But the wind wasn't blowing straight down the road anymore, it was striking the side of his face instead. The wind had done exactly as he had prayed for it to do all along, it had shifted back to blow from the north-west as before.

Canning still wouldn't believe it. Miracles didn't happen anywhere anymore, much less in the pitiless wasteland of the African Congo. But the breeze continued to cool his face, and continued to blow from the north-west, and slowly a sense of infinite relief washed over him. The wind had turned the path of the fire, and the flames were no longer chasing them but swerving away to the left of the road and heading away into the barrier of jungle and brush.

He looked back at Rona and said huskily, 'We made it, Lieutenant. We'll hump these cans a bit farther to make sure they're well out of the fire's reach, and then we'll just take one can on to the ambulance and come back for the rest.'

Rona still stared back at him uncertainly, 'What happens if — if the wind changes again?'

'It won't.' Canning was blindly and illogically sure that the wind would not change direction again.

Rona had no more breath left for argument and together they lifted up the cans and pushed onwards. However, now that the fire was no longer breathing down their necks to urge them on the reaction began to take effect on their strength-drained limbs and they both tottered on the verge of collapse. Rona had behaved incredibly well but now she was as close to exhaustion as Canning. They toiled for another three hundred yards and then Canning again stopped in the road.

'This will do,' he gasped. 'We'll leave three cans here.' As he spoke he knew that he had no real choice, for in their present state it would be an ordeal to carry even one can the rest of the way. They still had well over a mile to go.

Rona also realised that they had done all that was possible, and that now they would have to trust to fate and the whims of the breeze. They could carry the whole burden no further. She lowered her two cans wearily into the middle of the road and stood back breathing heavily as Canning placed one of his cans beside it. Then Canning took her reassuringly by the arm and they moved on, leaving the three hard-won cans behind.

Canning found that the one large, square can was almost as awkward to carry as two had been, for the weight pulled him over to one side now that there was nothing to balance it. He began to weave unsteadily to the side of the road and then Rona held back and pulled him to a stop.

'Get a stick — ' she said hoarsely, ' — and push it through the handle. We can carry it together.'

Canning realised that if they carried the can between them instead of stumbling along with its full weight dragging against his legs then they could progress far more easily, and he gave her a brief grateful smile.

'It's an idea,' he said. And then he lowered the can and walked over to the tangles of thicket that now flanked the road. He used his knife to chop down a stout branch and trimmed off the twigs with short, hacking strokes. Then he returned and pushed the branch through the handle of the can. Rona took the other end and they lifted together, moving off again with the can swaying between them.

They were able to move much faster now and made good time as they hurried along the moonlit road. Occasionally Canning glanced at the nurse's face, but Rona was concentrating her gaze on the dusty road surface some ten yards ahead and their eyes never met. He noticed the steady rise and fall of her breasts through the open blouse, the determined set of her face, and the grim silhouette made by the snout of the sten gun as it thrust above her right shoulder, and he wondered vaguely what she was thinking. They were so dependent upon each other now that he found it difficult to believe that only a few hours ago she had threatened him with a court martial.

They covered another half mile, and now, although the night sky behind them was still shrouded with smoke, they were well clear of the fire. And the wind still blew gently from the north-west. They could breathe properly and exhaustion was their only enemy. Canning's stubborn streak was still pushing him on but Rona's steps began to waver and several times she almost tripped on the uneven surface of the road.

Their progress became slower and Rona's shoulders began to sag, and

Canning feared that even now she was going to collapse completely before they reached the ambulance. Her steps became more faltering as she gamely tried to continue, and then Canning was granted his second miracle of the night.

There was a shuffle of footsteps from the road ahead and a dark shape moved uncertainly in the gloom. In the fraction of a second that followed, alarm triggered off a violent reaction in Canning's thumping heart, and then a hushed but familiar voice whispered urgently:

'Corp! Corp, is that you?'

Relief drained the tension from Canning's muscles like air hissing from a punctured rubber doll. He recognised the short, untidy figure with its white arm sling and the stained bandage round the ginger hair and said thankfully:

'It's all right, Morris. It's Lieutenant Waring and myself.'

Morris looked even more relieved than Canning had been as he came up to them out of the shadows.

He said breathlessly, 'Sergeant Hardman

sent me, Corp. He reckoned you might need some help on the last part of the way, and he said even one hand is better than none at all.'

Canning said with feeling, 'I love Sergeant Hardman, and I love you too. Take Lieutenant Waring's place will you, and give me a hand with this can.'

Morris was clumsily eager to please. He took Rona's end of the cut stick and again the petrol can was hoisted off the ground as they moved forward with hurrying steps. Rona trailed wearily behind them.

Twenty minutes later they were back at the ambulance and Canning was pouring the priceless four gallons of petrol into the empty tank. Hardman called him as he finished the job and he forced his tired limbs into fresh movement as he walked round to the back. Rona Waring was slumped against the open door, still on her feet but only just conscious, her chest rising and her eyes closed. Baxter and Delayney were still alert and Morris was resting at the far end.

Canning said, 'What is it, Sergeant?'

Hardman's eyes were active again, the only part of his crippled body that seemed really alive. He said weakly, 'You did a good job, Corporal. But where do you plan to go now?'

Canning rallied the reeling shreds of his aching mind and said slowly, 'It depends. There's a party of the Bantu still behind us, and I had hoped to drive through Sakinda and head north before the blacks could reorganise and return to the village. The road forks about three miles beyond Sakinda, right to join the Kangzi river, and left towards Ningini. But the damned fire got out of control, it didn't sweep on past Sakinda like I intended, but swung round and chased us half way back here. The wind has turned it away now, but it will be a long time before the ground behind it has cooled enough for us to drive through Sakinda. I think the only choice now is to pick up the cans of petrol I had to leave and then turn back for Kasuvu. We'll have to take a chance on running into the party that tried to head us off before.'

Hardman said weakly, 'It's a big risk. Those blacks must know that their friends have occupied Sakinda, and if they're capable of thinking for themselves at all they'll know that we must either be stopped there or turned back. And the chances are that they're laying another ambush on the Kasuvu road just to be sure.' The big Sergeant winced as another spasm of pain racked his shattered chest and then went on, 'But Ningini — that's different. There's another big detachment of U.N. troops there — mostly Ghurkas — and if Sergeant Riley got a radio message through at all we might even find them coming to meet us. It's a hundred and fifty miles, but if it's at all possible to get through Sakinda then Ningini is our best choice.'

Canning remembered the fury of the fire, but he trusted Hardman's judgment. He said grimly, 'All right, Sergeant. If it's humanly possible — I'll try.'

Nightmare Drive

Canning waited for half an hour before moving, partly to give the fire time to burn itself out along the road ahead, and partly because both he and Rona were hovering on the verge of collapse. They had to have a rest. Finally he stiffened his slumped body and struggled up slowly and painfully behind the wheel of the ambulance. Every bone and muscle in his body still ached with dull intensity and he had to grip the wheel with both hands in order to remain upright. Every nerve and sinew howled frantic radio messages to his brain in clamouring protest, and his smarting, half-closed eyes craved for sleep, but he knew that he had delayed as long as he dared and that now he must drive on. One way or another he had to get well clear of Sakinda before he could properly relax.

He glanced slowly at Rona Waring, she occupied the seat beside him, leaning heavily into the far corner of the cab with her head lolling on to her left shoulder. Her breathing was still strained and thrusting, but the lift of her breasts was more regular now. She looked as though she had sunk into a coma. Then she stirred feebly, her head lifted and she opened her eyes to look at him.

Canning said quietly, 'Go back to sleep, Lieutenant. There's not much else you can do.'

He tried the starter and the motor gave a spluttering whine. He tried again with the same result, and then on the third attempt the engine coughed, spluttered with a different note, and then swelled back to normality. Canning glanced back through the communication panel, but the back doors had been closed and he could see nothing in the pitch blackness. He guessed that Baxter and Delayney were still grimly clutching their sten guns with unseen hands, and he said softly:

'Hold tight, lads. We're moving off.'

Rona was now sitting upright beside him, watching as he moved the gears to set the ambulance in motion. She said nothing as the heavy vehicle began to roll slowly down the darkened road. The moon had floated into hiding behind some cloud and the African night was full of mysterious sound and deep shadows.

Canning drove without headlights, straining his eyes to follow the road ahead. After half a mile he picked out the vague shape of the three petrol cans he and Rona had been forced to leave behind and he braked slowly to a stop with his bonnet almost touching them. Rona stirred but he shook his head:

'Stay here, Lieutenant. I can manage.'

He got down from the cab and carried the three cans one at a time to the back of the ambulance. Morris gave him a hand to stack them as far back as possible out of the way. It was pointless to pour any more into the ambulance's tank for it would only waste away through the jagged spear hole. Finally Canning secured the back doors and returned to the cab again.

He drove on slowly, and soon he could again taste the first menacing swirls of smoke. His heart began to jitter but he kept going. The wind was unchanged and the fire had swept away to the south-east, but the road ahead was still thickly shrouded by smoke. Canning knew that although the charred bush on either side would still be smouldering, the road itself should be clear. The only real danger lay in the possibility of his being overcome by the smoke and the rolling heat waves still exuding from the blackened earth.

He stopped the ambulance and said slowly, 'Sure you won't change your mind, Lieutenant. It'll be grim up here, but the effects won't penetrate into the back quite so much.'

Rona smiled, 'I'll stay here with you.' She glanced down at his sten which lay between them and her lips framed a ghost of a smile. 'I don't suppose I could ever hit anything with it, but the blacks won't know that if we should bump into any at Sakinda. The noise might hold them off a bit.'

'All right.' Canning reached into his pocket and drew out two squares of torn sheet that he had ripped from Delayney's bed. He handed her one and said, 'Tie that tight round your mouth and nose, it's not a perfect fire-mask but it will filter some of the soot from your lungs. If I find that the going gets too tough I'll turn back.'

Rona accepted the torn sheet and he watched her tie it into place. Then he fixed his own mask and put the ambulance into gear once more. He knew that if anything went wrong during the next half-hour, if the ambulance should break down or blunder off the road to get stuck in the bush, or if he himself was to collapse, then it would mean a slow death from asphyxiation for everyone aboard. But despite the risk he still had faith in Hardman's judgment, and he drove slowly into the black fog that filled the road.

After a few seconds he switched on his headlights to cut a path through the swirling smoke; already the cloud had filled the cab and was prickling hotly into their eyes, making the tears trickle once more down their faces. On either side little bursts of yellow flame still flickered where a stubborn bush still burned in the fire's wake. The heat was suffocating, the very air blistered and scorched. The road was a frail ribbon of red dust between the flanking sides of blackened earth, the dead stubble that had once been grassland smouldered and crackled. Canning put his foot down and drove as fast as he dared, knowing that he had to get through this nightmare landscape as quickly as possible, but at the same time horribly aware of how easy it would be for the ambulance to break an axle or else crash into a pot-hole and spin off the road.

Canning had once seen a painting of hell; an inferno of scarlet flames and screaming demons, of horned tails and stabbing pitchforks, and white bodies twisting through open furnace doors; everything starkly clear in violent crimson and glowing reds. But the painting had been wrong, and the artist had had no conception at all of the reality of hell. Hell was not stark and clear in glowing colours. Hell was a blackened wasteland, swirling in smoke and drowned by night. Hell was a raw burning in the lungs, tortured coughing and strangling fingers about your throat. Hell was not a burst of flame and a crisp, sizzling end; hell was slow suffocation, an obscured nightmare wreathed in smoke and the taste of retching, lingering death. Hell was nothing like that painting at all; except, perhaps, for the demons. And even the demons lacked tails and pitchforks, and were simply flickers of yellow flame that danced in and out of the smoke along the sides of the road, grinning and taunting, and beckoning with evil fingers.

Canning was half-blind and near helpless, his senses reeling as the poisonous fumes seeped into his brain. His body was drenched in fresh sweat and he was fighting for air beneath the white mask that covered his face. Rona had doubled forwards with her head between her knees and was gagging pitifully and he could hear more choking coughing from the wounded men in the back. He knew he should have turned back. They couldn't make it and they would all die. But it was too late now to turn back. They were half-way there and beyond the point of no return. It was Sakinda or die.

He could sense unconsciousness reaching out to claim him and in desperation he put his foot hard down. It didn't matter now whether they crashed or the axle broke, for unless he took suicide risks then death was horribly certain. The ambulance surged forward, the headlights almost useless in the twisting black fog. She bounced and lurched over gulleys and pot-holes, miraculously sticking to the thin sliver of the road. Canning hung blindly to the wheel and prayed.

A burning thicket loomed out of the darkness, still inhabited by waltzing candle-flames of yellow fire. Canning realised that here the road turned and pulled hard at the wheel to make the bend. The wheels slewed through the dust and the side of the heavy vehicle slammed into the dying thicket, smashing off the brittle, blackened branches. Canning pulled her straight again and roared the engine with insane pressure on the accelerator. He could feel his senses slipping away, submerging into the endless darkness of eternity. And then suddenly he was breaking out of the wasteland and racing into Sakinda.

Hope dragged him back from the edge of unconsciousness. The smoke was clearing and he was through the desolation of scorched earth and scattered fires; he was through the sea of poisoned fumes and the hideous snap and crackling of burning branches. He was back in the empty compound of Sakinda and driving away from the merciless oven of heat.

He drove straight through the village, thankful that Rona was still spent and doubled up beside him, and unable to look up at the gruesome decorations on the three big trees. He headed the ambulance into the gap in the jungle that marked the entrance to the road north and wasted no time in putting the village behind him.

There was no trace of the fire here and the air was blessedly smoke-free, and luxuriously cool. Canning tore the white mask away from his mouth and sucked in delicious gulps of air as he steadied the wheel with one hand. Rona rallied a little and lifted her head unsteadily to face the draught of cold air that swept through the empty windscreen, and he reached over to pull her fire-mask down past her chin. Her eyes were terribly bloodshot and she was still struggling wretchedly to breathe, but somehow she forced him the feeblest attempt at a smile.

The headlights showed up the road ahead clearly now, and the moon had re-appeared to filter a few pale rays through the branches of the trees. They were no longer travelling through brush and savannah but had been swallowed up by the jungle barrier. Close tangles of fern and bamboo lined the road, and beyond an unseen network of vines and creepers brooded in the inky blackness.

Canning slowed the ambulance and turned his head towards the black slit of the communication panel.

'Is everyone all right in there?' he demanded.

There was a moment's silence, and then Baxter's voice came weakly, 'I'm all right, Corp. But I think the others have passed out. It's still a bit stuffy in here.'

Canning stopped the ambulance and stumbled out. He almost fell to his knees and had to hang on to the cab door for momentary support. Then he pushed himself away and went round to the back. He pulled the double doors wide open to let the night air replace the trapped remnants of swirling smoke that were still inside. Only Baxter still sat up. Morris had collapsed on the floor behind him and the others lay unmoving on their beds.

Rona appeared beside him, her eyes were almost hidden by great red circles and her body was slow with fatigue. She said weakly:

'There should be a torch in the emergency kit. I'll get it.'

Canning helped her into the ambulance and then climbed in after her. He waited beside Baxter while she fumbled for the torch and then they both bent over Morris who had crumpled up on the floor, his head strangely twisted and jammed up against the petrol cans. For one horrible second they thought that Morris had fallen and broken his neck, but then the light of the torch showed that he was still breathing sluggishly and that his head was just pushed to one side by the cans. They straightened him up and left him on the floor, borrowing one of Baxter's pillows to prop beneath his head. Both Delayney and Garner were unconscious in their beds but were breathing well, and when they turned to Hardman the big Sergeant's eyes had flickered open.

He said painfully, 'I guess we must have made it, Corporal. Otherwise you wouldn't have stopped.'

'We made it, Sarge.' Canning tried to keep his voice level as he spoke. 'I'll make another couple of miles to put us properly clear of Sakinda, and then we'll park for the night. Night driving is too dangerous on these imitation roads, and we're all bushed anyway.'

Hardman's eyes registered approval. 'Go ahead, Corporal.'

Canning turned to Rona, 'There's nothing else you can do here for the moment. Are you coming back to the cab?'

She nodded and he helped her down.

They left the doors swinging open so that the fresh air could revive the unconscious men, and a few moments later they were on their way again.

Canning drove for just over a mile and then the fork in the road suddenly appeared in the range of the headlights. He slowed the ambulance and bore left, following the single arm of the signpost that said simply NINGINI 196 klms. 196 kilometres was approximately 147 miles.

He drove another half mile and then stopped, pulling the ambulance into a small clearing of shrub and fern that was almost an overgrown lay-by at the side of the road. He stared dully at the forbidding wall of vines and jungle that now loomed directly ahead and then switched off the engine. The sudden silence was hushed and oppressive. He switched off the lights and the inrush of darkness was even worse.

He commanded the nurse to wait and then descended once more from his cab. He waded through knee-deep bracken to reach the back of the ambulance, and after making sure that there was nothing

251

else to be done for his patients he closed and locked the doors. Then he returned to his cab and wound up the side window, telling Rona to do the same on her side. There was nothing he could do about the empty windscreen, but at least he felt secure from anything bigger than mosquitoes and snakes. He suppressed a shuddering picture of a python wending its way over the bonnet and hissing into their faces during the night and turned to speak to Rona who was invisible in the darkness.

'Try and get some sleep, Lieutenant. The Bantu won't get organised until dawn, and I doubt if they'd wander about the jungle at night anyway. We should be safe enough here.'

But there was no answer from Rona Waring, she had already succumbed to the sweeping tide of exhaustion.

Canning leaned back in his seat, his eyes closing and his hand resting on the sten gun between them. He wondered vaguely whether there was an army law forbidding the sharing of sleeping quarters with a female officer, but the thought was drowned as he too sank into the enveloping blanket of darkness.

★ ★ ★

It was dawn when Canning awoke, the angled rays of the rising sun were glancing through the maze of branches and vines and spreading dappled patches of green-gold light over the carpet of bracken that covered the clearing. There was a host of bird life flittering on coloured wings, and a score of chattering monkeys leaping from creeper to creeper; all curious but wary of the strange, square steel animal that had appeared in their midst. The jungle was full of squeaks and rustles, the shrill cries of the birds, and, from somewhere deep and distant among the shadowed boles, the suspicious grunting of a wild pig.

Canning was awakened by the warmth of the sun, together with a deep-planted inner compulsion that warned him that it was dangerous to linger in the daylight. He still felt the gruelling effects of the previous day and his body was just one great, congealed mass of aches. His eyes were still glued together by weariness and his mouth was burning up with thirst. His back-bone wasn't bone anymore but flexible sponge rubber that would never hold his weight again. He wanted to sink back into the sweet luxury of unconsciousness but vague memories of blood and killing, and of fire and hell and helpless men slowly dominated his mind. He struggled upright and miraculously the sponge-rubber back-bone did support him. He made another effort and pushed open his gummed eyes.

Rona Waring still slumped back on her seat beside him. She looked small and dirty, her clothes rumpled and stained with sweat and soot, her blonde hair streaked with black smudges and falling down over her face. She was still fast asleep and her buttonless blouse had refused to stay closed over her rising breasts in their black lace bra. She looked nothing at all like the chic little baby doll nurse with the wide bue eyes who had left Kasuvu such a long, long time ago. Canning smiled somewhat bitterly and wondered what sort of a picture he made in turn. He didn't really like to think about it. Stiffly Canning climbed down from the cab and went back to examine the men in the rear of the ambulance. He found Baxter and Morris both fast asleep on the floor, but Hardman and Delayney were both awake. Garner's temperature had dropped and he appeared to be sleeping peacefully at last.

Canning made sure that they were all comfortable and lingered for a quiet, reassuring word with the two men who lay awake. There was nothing else he could do then but return to his cab and drive on, for he had no food or water to give them until they reached Ningini.

Rona woke with a jolt as he started the engine and there was sudden fear in her eyes as she struggled upright. Her face was pale and her whole body trembled.

Canning said, 'Sorry, Lieutenant. I didn't mean to bring you out of dreamland like that. I thought you'd sleep through it.' He hesitated with his hand on the gear lever and then said, 'I've already looked over the men. You can get some more sleep.'

Rona still looked pasty, 'I'd rather not, Corporal.' She looked at him with faltering eyes and added, 'It wasn't a very pleasant dream.'

Canning watched her as she turned her face away and rubbed a tired hand over her eyes, and something inside him seemed to weaken. He said quietly:

'By nightfall we'll be in Ningini, Lieutenant, and then that's all it will all be — just a dream.'

Rona straightened herself and tried to smile, 'I hope you're right, Corporal. I only hope you're right.'

Canning could think of nothing else to say, and after a moment's hesitancy he put the gear lever into reverse and backed the ambulance out on to the road once more. A sweet smell of sap rose from the crushed ferns, but then it faded behind them as the ambulance nosed along the jungle road to Ningini.

The miles lengthened behind them and Canning became gradually more cheerful;

but his spirits would have been far less buoyant if he could have known that by nightfall he would not be safe in Ningini, but would again be re-tracing his route to the death trap of Sakinda.

Hours of Tension

Canning drove in silence with his attention centred on the road ahead, maintaining as even a speed as possible over the rutted surface. Tall jungle formed a wall on either side, the wrinkled boles of the big trees standing solid in the strangling embrace of fern, vines and bush. The nearer leaves were a glossy, sun-bright green, becoming dull green and then dark green, and finally green-black as the eye penetrated the sombre gloom of the depths. The air was alive with noise and birds, and sharp spears of sunlight flashing through the upper branches where the monkeys paused in play to watch the ambulance lumber past below them. The road behind was full of dust clouds and the road ahead splashed with blotches of sunshine and flickers of shadow.

Canning drove in silence because he had nothing to say. He was heavily conscious of Rona's presence in the cab beside him but he did not look at her. She had pulled the unruly edges of her blouse together once more and from somewhere had produced a comb to bring some vague sense of order to her blonde hair; she was now sitting almost erect with her left arm lodged in the open window. Her eyes were still dulled with traces of tiredness as she listlessly watched the passing foliage. She had not spoken since they had regained the road and Canning sensed that somehow the old barrier was stealthily edging its way back between them.

He wondered what she was thinking, if anything at all. Was she still mourning Holland, or was she reliving the past night of fire; was she planning his court martial, or merely dreaming wistfully of water for her parched throat. He couldn't guess and he couldn't ask, and he told himself that it didn't really matter anyway. Probably she was too tired to think of anything and her mind was a blank. He wished her luck. He wished his own mind would go mercifully blank.

The road wound untidily between the twin barriers of forest, and yesterday's enemies, the heat and the dust, came back to add fresh misery to his sluggish thoughts. His mouth, throat, lungs and stomach were thickly lined by the fine red dust that was churned up by their trundling wheels, and he wondered how his body could possibly continue to function with so much muck in the works. He tried to remember what beer tasted like, and then tried even harder not to remember because memory could only bring torment and never relief.

The miles registered with maddening slowness on the speedometer clock, each increasing figure on the dial taking longer to roll upwards into view than the one before. The sun was climbing higher to flood them with the full fury of its blazing rays and the flanking jungle was no longer such an effective shield. Canning's limbs were stiff and cramped and fresh sweat was again spreading through his soiled clothes. He already smelled strongly and he knew it, and he wondered again whether he was offending the nurse's dainty nostrils. Then he grinned somewhat bitterly and decided that she was not exactly wearing 'Ashes of Roses' herself.

Gradually the miles behind them lengthened, until after three hours of driving they were nearly fifty miles from Sakinda. Canning scowled at the speedo needle that wavered hesitantly around the twenty mark, and told himself sourly that on a good road he could have covered the same distance in an hour. But not by any stretch of the imagination could the roads of Africa be described as good; at least, not in this part of the Congo. For every hundred yards where he could maintain a steady average of speed there was another hundred yards of sprawling roots, holes and gulleys, and with a full load of badly injured men he did not dare jolt them about more than was absolutely necessary. A haemorrhage had killed Jack Foster and could quite easily do the same to Hardman. It was impossible to hurry.

Canning looked down again at the mileage gauge on the speedometer clock and promised himself that as soon as it had registered the first fifty miles he would stop and rest. He needed a rest badly for every joint was knotted up with cramp and his backside had long ago gone numb with the aching discomfort of sitting in a pool of his own sweat. He knew that the men behind him must also be craving relief from the interminable bumping and lurching of the ambulance, and it was time that the nurse checked them over anyway. Morris had been instructed to keep an eye on the feverish Garner and to give a shout if help was needed, but Morris was probably suffering as much as the rest; even though the little man's shattered arm did not render him as near totally helpless as the others it must be causing him at least as much pain as Delayney's thigh or Baxter's foot and ankle.

The road dipped into a narrow ravine, a red gash through walls of sandstone rock. The jungle still grew densely on either side but at the bottom of the ravine there was nothing but hard sand and an occasional patch of scrub huddling close to the walls. The figures on the mileage gauge began to roll upwards to register the completion of the first fifty miles, and Canning told himself grimly that he had covered a third of the journey, and even if the road did not improve he would still be rolling into Ningini in some six hours time. He did not consider that the road might become worse, for any further deterioration seemed impossible.

However, the promised break had to wait, for here the ravine had formed a broiling trap for the sun's rays and the heat was murderous; it enveloped them in a shimmering haze that sucked the sweat from their bodies like hot steam. The rust red walls seemed to join together where the ravine turned a sudden bend ahead and Canning slowed down as he approached it. Here the ravine was deeper than the ambulance, but the floor was beginning to slope up again and Canning hoped that once round the bend the road would climb out of it. He steered round the bend and his hopes crashed headlong into the dust as he was forced to brake sharply, slamming both feet hard down on brake and clutch to avoid the barrier of fallen rock that blocked his path.

Rona sat bolt upright beside him and Canning instinctively scooped up his sten gun from the seat between them. His eyes searched the edges of the ravine above and there was a sick feeling in his stomach as he thrust the sten through the few edges of glass that still clung to the frame of the windscreen. Then slowly the first violent rush of fear began to fade as the silence lengthened. The ambulance had stalled as Canning had braked but there was no outburst of gunfire to replace the roaring of its engine in the confined spaces of the ravine. There were no shrieking Bantu war cries, no naked black soldiers swarming above the jagged crest of the rockfall. There was no ambush.

Rona pulled her eyes away from the dead-end in front of them and looked helplessly at Canning as he drew the sten gun back into the cab. Her throat muscles worked as though she was searching for words, but words failed her and she could only stare with bitter, empty eyes.

Canning bit back the futile tide of savage curses that were slowly rising in his throat and pushed open the door of the cab. To Rona he said harshly:

'Stay here, Lieutenant.'

She made no answer but watched him dumbly as he climbed down into the road. He still kept the sten in his hand as he slammed the door and moved forward to inspect the barrier. The heat drowned him and the fierce glare from the red rock made him screw his eyelids until he was squinting through barest slits. He studied the edges of the ravine yet again, staring upwards with his muscles tensed and the sten ready to swing up instantly in his hands. He was suspicious, distrustful, and almost certain that this had to be Larocque's doing; but there was no sound and no movement to disturb the heat-heavy stillness among the rocks.

He approached the landslide cautiously; the whole of one side of the ravine had torn away, blocking the way completely. The rock had broken off in great chunks as though it had been blasted out by dynamite. Then Canning saw the great grey roots that poked above the mass of debris like stiffened tendrils probing the air. He relaxed a fraction and used one hand to steady himself as he climbed up over the rocks and rubble. When he reached the top he could look down upon the great tree trunk that filled the ravine beyond, its crushed and broken branches spreading in a tangle of smashed greenery from wall to wall.

He did swear then, slowly and with infinite bitterness. For year after year that massive giant of the forest must have balanced on the very lip of the ravine, towering above the road while its huge roots probed through the red earth and finally penetrated the shallow cracks in the rock; penetrating deeper and deeper and splitting the rock wall gradually apart until a gust of wind or splintering of a widening crack had brought it crashing down. The process of growth and the gradual crumbling of the rocky wall of the ravine must have taken countless years, but through sheer filthy luck the end had come during the last two days to bar his route to Ningini.

Wearily Canning flexed his aching shoulders as he surveyed the situation through sun-dazzled eyes. Only a crane would lift that massive, sprawling tree trunk, and nothing short of a giant bulldozer would be able to clear the avalanche of rock that had been wrenched out as the tree toppled and fell. Ningini had suddenly vanished from a six-hour drive to the other side of the moon. He turned away and climbed slowly back down the slope to the ambulance.

Rona had dropped down from the cab and now moved hesitantly to meet him.

'Can you clear it, Corporal?' she asked hopelessly. 'Can you clear enough to get through?'

Canning looked into her face and said quietly, 'It's impossible, Lieutenant. I couldn't clear a path wide enough to wheel a bicycle through, much less that bloody great ambulance.'

Rona flinched, 'I'm sorry, Corporal. I — I suppose it should have been obvious.'

Canning forced a smile, and he was

suddenly aware that now that they were in trouble again their own personal barrier seemed to be fading away.

'Let's climb back into the cab and reverse out of this sweat-box,' he said. 'The road's absolutely impassable and there's nothing we can do by just staring at it. And I can't think while I'm being roasted alive.'

Rona looked into his eyes for a moment, and was slightly reassured by the solid determination that was still reflected in their grey depths. She nodded her head in a weary sign of agreement and then turned back to her side of the cab. Canning pulled open his own door and heaved his stocky frame behind the wheel. He waited until she was settled beside him and then put the gear lever into reverse and backed up round the bend in the ravine.

Rona continued to stare at the receding barrier until the curving rock walls gradually merged together to close it from view. The dead tangle of roots thrusting above the ridge of rocks were all that she could see of the fallen tree and then even they were hidden by the narrowing gap. She turned to look at Canning but all that she could see was his back and shoulders as he hung half-out of the cab to watch the road behind him, and suddenly the memory of his determined eyes was not so reassuring any more. The road to Ningini was hopelessly blocked and she was conscious more than ever before of the fact that her lips were dry and cracked and her mouth was horribly thirsty; and, what was worse, the sick men behind her must be suffering equally as badly. Where could they hope to find water now?

There was no room to turn and Canning backed the ambulance all the way out of the ravine. He was driving back into his own dust cloud and breathed nothing but the fine, choking red powder all the way. His eyes were half-closed but still clogged full of grit and by the time he was able to straighten up again and face the front he was so dizzy that he was almost fainting from the heat.

He had to relax for a few moments

to force the weariness away from his complaining limbs, and then he had to blink repeatedly before the tears washed the dust out of his bloodshot eyes. Rona was watching him with a worried expression on her face and he forced her a fleeting grin. At the same time he was suddenly aware of how much concentrated effort each new grin was beginning to need.

'I'll turn her around,' he said. 'And then we'll take a break and have a look at the lads in the back before we drive any farther.'

Rona was silent for a moment, then she asked dully:

'Where to?'

Canning's face tightened up, and no amount of effort could force a grin this time. He said grimly:

'I don't know. But I can only think of one choice.'

He pulled himself closer to the wheel again and pushed the gear lever into first, locking the wheels hard over to one side. He had to shunt the heavy ambulance backwards and forwards several times before he could turn her completely round in the narrow road to face back to Sakinda. Then he drove forward a few hundred yards to reach the shade of two stout cedars that rose above the rest of the jungle that flanked the road, and there he stopped. They both got down into the road and met at the back of the ambulance.

Canning pulled the doors open and helped the nurse inside. Four pairs of eyes watched them enter and then Rona said quietly:

'How are you feeling, boys?'

No one answered, and then Hardman said:

'Morris took a look through the communication panel the first time we stopped. He tells us that the road through the ravine is blocked.' He paused for a moment as his eyes searched for Canning, then he went on, 'What's the situation, Corporal?'

Canning saw no point in being gentle. He said flatly:

'Morris was right. The road is blocked. There isn't a hope in hell of getting through it, and the jungle is far too thick to try and drive round the top of the ravine. We've got no choice but to turn back.'

'To Sakinda!' Delayney's exclamation was half question and half protest.

'Almost to Sakinda.' Canning's voice was blunt, 'We'll have to go back as far as the fork a mile from the village and then swing left along the Kangzi. There's another turn-off about eighty miles along that road that will bring us back to Ningini again. It's a much longer trip, but we should have just enough petrol to make it.'

Hardman's teeth gritted together and his face tightened under the bloodless skin. 'If you swing along the Kangzi you'll be moving farther away from U.N. controlled territory, right into the heart of rebel Katanga. You'll have to go almost back to Sakinda which is dangerous enough, but after that you'll have to pass through several more villages where we could be stopped. And bush telegraph is much faster than we are. It's a big risk all along the line.'

'I've thought of all that, Sarge, but I still haven't any alternative. We can't possibly get through this road, and neither can we stay here. We must go back. It's practically suicide to try and run the gauntlet of Sakinda again and get back on the Kasuvu road — and the only other way is to turn along the Kangzi.'

* * *

Canning had no intention of nearing Sakinda once more in broad daylight, and so they were forced to simply wait and do nothing for the rest of the long hot hours before late afternoon. Rona Waring did what little she could in the way of fixing fresh bandages for the wounded men, but as she had nothing left to use but torn sheets the finished effects looked somewhat clumsy. There was no water and no food, and they could do nothing but attempt to ignore the knifing pains of hunger and thirst. The injured men slept fitfully through the sticky heat, and Rona and Canning took

273

it in turn to do likewise. The motionless Garner was still in a deep coma on the top bed, and although his fever had abated Rona was more worried about his condition than anything else. She wasn't quite sure what kind of tropical fever Garner had been suffering from, and even in their present unenvious situation the unknown was just a little bit more disturbing than the known.

At last the tension-filled hours of waiting were over, and Canning grimly roused himself and picked up his sten. He shielded his eyes to squint towards the declining sun and satisfied himself that by the time he was again approaching Sakinda it would be dusk. He looked at Rona and said quietly:

'It's time to go, Lieutenant.'

Rona stood up, smoothing down her crumpled skirt and straightening the kahki blouse that was beginning to gape open. Then she looked at him levelly and held her hand out for the sten. Canning released it without argument, for the argument was already over. He had told her that on the return trip she would be travelling in the back with the injured where there would be less danger if they did run into more of Larocque's Bantu soldiery on the road; but Rona had refused and insisted that she could do a more valuable job by riding in the cab to cover him if necessity arose. There had been no mention of rank — if there had been Canning would not have finally given way — instead she had argued her point with logic and common sense, and won. Canning was still not entirely happy, but stubbornness did not stop him from realising that it would be criminal stupidity to get himself shot at the wheel as Spencer had been. He needed someone to distract the Bantu's attention from himself, even if it did have to be the nurse.

They locked the rear doors, despite a murmur of protest from Delayney, who, with Baxter, had again pulled close his own gun, and then they returned to the cab. Canning started the engine and they began the fifty mile drive back to Sakinda.

The sun sank lower in a sky of fire

and the tension gradually mounted as the miles rolled past, each turn of the wheels twisting the knots tighter in Canning's stomach. The first hours passed and dusk began to gather. The sun died in a barely-noticed pageant of glowing colour, and Sakinda was only a few miles ahead in the thickening gloom.

Night on the Kangzi

There was no conversation on the return trip; Canning and Rona had once again donned their habitual mantle of silence, and a combination of discomforting thirst, pain and tightened nerves robbed the men in the back of all desire to talk. The African night fell swiftly once the sun had set, and tonight there were thick clouds obscuring the moon. Canning switched on his side lights to relieve the darkness and drove in third gear with his foot depressing the accelerator as lightly as possible. He didn't want full headlights making a great slash of light through the jungle and he was striving the keep engine noise to a minimum. The mileage gauge told him that he was less than a mile from the spot where he had started out that morning.

Occasionally he glanced at Rona on the seat beside him, she was leaning forward slightly, her lips compressed and her eyes straining into the night; her hands never strayed from the sten gun that nestled in her lap. He studied her surreptitiously and suddenly decided that she didn't look like Jenny any more. It was impossible to picture the immaculate Jenny without make-up, with her lips cracked and her clothes sweat-stained, and with smudges of soot and dust streaking her lovely blonde hair. He realised with a slight sense of surprise that he had unconsciously stopped comparing the two girls in his mind. He had to, for it was impossible to imagine Jenny firing the bush upwind of Sakinda in the middle of the African night; it was impossible to imagine Jenny struggling beside him to out-race the hungry flames with the incredibly heavy cans of petrol; impossible to picture her determinedly tending injured men when she was half-dead from exhaustion herself. And even now, as he glanced beside him, it was impossible to see anything of Jenny in the tired girl with the sten gun in the lap of her skirt. Rona Waring had taken on a personality of her own.

The ambulance crawled past the clearing of crushed bracken where they had parked the previous night, and Canning almost failed to recognise it in the gloom beyond the feeble glow of his side lights. The realisation that they were almost back to the fork in the road made him harness his thoughts and concentrate more grimly on probing the darkness ahead. He knew that by now the fire of the previous night must have passed on or burnt out, and that it was most likely that Larocque's Bantu would have re-occupied the village. It was also probable that the small party who had attempted to stop them on the Kasuvu road would have tired of awaiting their return and rejoined the main band, and Larocque would know that somewhere the ambulance had given him the slip. The mercenary would realise that the ambulance must keep to the roads, and if he suspected that they had doubled back through Sakinda under cover of the fire then he would know from the lack of reports from the Katangan controlled villages along the Kangzi that they must have headed for Ningini. And if by foul chance Larocque knew that the Ningini road was impassable then it was quite possible that he was calmly waiting for them to return on the road ahead. Canning could only drive on and hope, and pray that Larocque had assumed that the ambulance had somehow dodged his tribesmen on the Kasuvu road and escaped south, or that the mercenary was unaware of the landslide that had blocked the ravine.

The surrounding jungle was again an invisible backcloth of menacing noise. The weak glimmer of the side lights barely illuminated the road immediately beneath the bonnet and the night was shrouded in rustling darkness. The moon was still trapped behind a ridge of clouds and only the faintest suggestion of relief marked the strip of open sky above them. The tension was verging on unbearable and Canning was horribly afraid that the sharp, jungle-trained ears of some of the natives at Sakinda might pick up the alien sound of their engine in the night. The thought made him slacken his foot even more from the accelerator pedal, crawling the ambulance forward at near stalling pace as he endeavoured to cut down even more on engine noise.

Suddenly and unexpectedly they were at the fork, and the faint outline of the single signpost was just discernible in the gloom. Canning fumbled with the steering wheel and swallowed hard with relief as he pulled left on to the Kangzi road, at the same time he could not quell the urge to glance quickly to his right where the last mile of invisible road led to Sakinda. There was no sound in the blackness that did not match the normal rustlings of the jungle, and no signs of the feared ambush. They began to crawl, still at near stalling speed in the new direction, and each ponderous turn of the wheels took them slowly away from the fork, away from the enemy camp of Sakinda.

Canning began to relax and the tension eased reluctantly away from his tightened muscles. His stomach settled and his nerves began to return to normal. He glanced across at Rona and said softly:

'That's the biggest hurdle over.'

Rona's face was deeply etched with lines of strain and her cheeks showed up palely even in the gloom. The breath escaped slowly from her lungs and she replaced it as though this was the first time she had breathed for long minutes. She had to draw another breath before she could speak and then her voice was low and half-suppressed in her throat.

'What happens next? Are you going to drive on all night?'

'I wish I could.' His voice had hardened bitterly, 'but it's just too bloody chancy. It was a necessary evil to get past Sakinda, but on these roads it would be too easy to break an axle or smash up the ambulance altogether in the darkness. I'll put a few safe miles behind us and then we'll have to lay up again until daylight. We'll just have to pray that there are no more terrorist bands or Katangan troops resident at any of the villages we have to crash through tomorrow.'

Rona looked doubtful. 'Those men behind us are badly hurt, and I haven't been able to give them a drink since yesterday morning. They haven't asked for any yet, because they know I have nothing to give, but they must be suffering agonies of thirst. Some of them might not last another day.'

Canning said, 'I'm sorry, Lieutenant, but I still can't risk crashing the ambulance by driving on in the dark. If the first village we come to tomorrow isn't too heavily populated I'll try and get food and water at the point of my sten. That's the best I can do.'

Rona hesitated, and then said quietly, 'I'm sorry too, Corporal. I know you're doing everything that's possible.'

Canning felt vaguely uncomfortable as he turned his head to meet her eyes. He said:

'We'll make it somehow. Our luck must change soon, and it can't possibly change for the worse.'

She smiled at him in the gloom and then they drove on in silence once more. Canning risked speeding up a little now that there was no danger of the engine being heard in Sakinda and he switched his headlights on to full. Then, after a cautious six miles of driving he saw the black gleam of water ahead. The moon had slipped away from the clouds to relieve the darkness and he realised that the road had wound its way into a low valley to follow the course of the Kangzi river. Here the road ran almost on to the river bank before winding away again into the jungle, and Canning steered the ambulance into the jungle's edge to stop for the night.

For a moment there was a hushed silence as he switched off the engine, he stared through the intervening network of trees and branches that now separated them from the Kangzi and listened to the soft rush of the river as it swirled through the shallows around the sandbanks. Then he turned to Rona and said slowly:

'We were just worrying about water, Lieutenant. But there's all we'll ever need out there. Dare we drink it?' He was aware of the parched constriction in his throat as he spoke and tried not to make his voice sound too eager.

Rona licked her dried lips and then answered equally slowly:

'Normally, no. It could be full of

typhoid, blackwater and God knows what else. But those men in the back need water badly, and in the circumstances we could take the risk. If it's not too dirty the risk is justifiable.'

'Then let's find out,' Canning grinned suddenly. 'We're not exactly over-fed and well-refreshed ourselves, are we?'

She smiled back and together they climbed out of the cab. Rona left the sten behind on the seat but Canning automatically picked it up again before following her round to the back of the ambulance.

★ ★ ★

An hour later the clouds had dispersed and the moon once more ruled the black vastness of the heavens, the stars laid a vapour trail of glowing sparks across the night sky and the whisper of crickets' wings filled the soft air. The ambulance was hidden by the dense black shadows of the jungle but the moving bosom of the Kangzi was faintly visible in the dim light. From somewhere downstream on the far bank came the heavy splashing and shrill trumpeting that could only mean that a small herd of elephant had come out of the forest to drink, and away on their left a hyena barked plaintively as he roamed his scavenging way through the night.

Canning stood with his back resting against the bonnet of the ambulance, his sten gun was close at hand and standing upright against the wheel. His mouth still retained the slightly brackish taste of the small cupful of river water that had barely shifted the dust from his throat, but even for that he was grateful. At this point the Kangzi was fast flowing and reasonably clean and they had drunk sparingly of the single water-bottle that Canning had filled. Rona had again tended the wounded men and made them as comfortable as possible for the night after eking out a few mouthfuls of water to each, and now they had settled down to get what small amount of sleep they could. Rona had climbed back into the cab and Canning had elected to stand guard for the first part of the night.

Despite the cat-naps he had snatched during the day his eyes were heavy and he shifted position often to keep himself awake. He had to constantly remind himself that the Bantu were not scattered and fleeing in confusion before the fire as they had been the previous night, and that consequently it was vital that he remained alert. By this time Larocque must have the tribesmen organised again, and if by ill-chance the noise of the ambulance had been heard as they sneaked past Sakinda, then the mercenary might have sent his Congolese soldiers in pursuit. And at this stage Canning was not willing to leave anything to chance.

It became increasingly difficult to keep his eyes open, and after a time Canning picked up his sten and moved quietly towards the river. He had not yet seen a single crocodile, but he knew that most Central African rivers were infested with the scaly reptiles and so he stepped more warily as he neared the bank. A chorus of frogs set up a croaking serenade somewhere in the reeds and he slapped softly as one of the myriad of buzzing flies settled on his face. He listened for a moment, and from far away the rasping cough of a hunting leopard was borne down-river on the slight breeze.

The ground became marshy and then he was standing on the very edge of the river bank. He knelt quietly and laid the sten on the dew-wet grass, cupping his hands into the shallow water to douse his face. He washed some of the caked dust from his arms and felt refreshed. Then he straightened up and told himself that he was fit to resume guard duty, and in the same second a reed snapped with a brittle popping sound behind him.

Canning spun round, still kneeling and still balanced on his toes. His out-stretched hand flashed towards his sten and in the same moment his legs became crossed and he sat down heavily on his backside. The sten was already in his hands but he lowered it as he recognised the silhouette of Rona Waring.

'I'm sorry, Corporal,' she said quietly. 'I should have called out to warn you instead of sneaking up behind you like that.'

Canning managed to untangle his legs and struggle slowly upright, breathing heavily and still clinging like a limpet to his sten. He said brusquely:

'Why aren't you sleeping while you've got the chance? You're not supposed to relieve me for another three hours.'

'I couldn't sleep.' She moved a little closer through the reeds. 'I think I dozed too much during the day. Or perhaps I'm worrying too much about tomorrow.' She hesitated uncertainly, her expression lost behind the falling shadows cast by the nearer tangles of jungle. 'Besides, I — I wanted to talk to you.'

Canning's smile was vaguely bitter in the darkness. 'Strange, isn't it, Lieutenant. A couple of days ago you threatened me with a court martial — tonight you want moonlight conversation. Life is funny that way.'

She stiffened and he could sense the anger pulsing through her frame. He knew that he was being unfair, and childishly hurtful, but although his earlier animosity had gone he still could not quite change his attitude on the surface.

Rona said harshly, 'Corporal, you are the most resentful, sullen, insolent, downright surly example of a soldier that I've ever met. You took an instant dislike to me from the moment we met and you've done your damnedest to show it in every possible way. But surely not even you can believe that I'd be spiteful enough to push a court martial charge after all we've been through in the last two days.'

Canning flinched and it was several moments before he could meet her gaze. When he did he felt as though she was looking down at him instead of up. He said slowly:

'No, Lieutenant. I didn't believe you'd go through with a court martial. I didn't even believe it at the time.' He paused, 'I'm sorry.'

He turned and stared away down the moving black surface of the river, hoping that she would accept his apology and return to the ambulance. He felt disgusted with his own behaviour but he didn't know how to redeem it. He ignored the buzzing of the mosquitoes and waited for the sound of her retreating footsteps through the reeds.

But there was no movement from behind. Rona was standing her ground and waiting until he was ready to face her once more.

He had to turn back and face her.

She said quietly, 'Corporal, can I ask you something?'

He hesitated, 'Go ahead.'

She said carefully, 'What is it that causes that great big chip on your shoulder? At first I thought that it was my rank, a resentment towards authority, or just plain pig-headedness towards anything with more than two stripes. But it's not that. I've noticed the way you listen to Hardman. That half-dead Sergeant knows his job and you respect him for it — you respect his opinion. So it's not just a matter of rank-distinction. So — what is it with me?'

There was a long silence. Canning stood with the sten gun in one hand and the other arm hanging limply at his side, and found that he couldn't pull his eyes away from the nurse's frank gaze. He knew that he owed her an explanation; after all they had been through together he owed her much, much more than an explanation. But at the same time the words fought to stay locked in his mind.

Then Rona said softly, very softly indeed:

'Who was she? What was her name?'

'Her name was Jenny.' The answer had burst the restraining barrier before he could hold it back and he found himself talking on. 'Her name was Jenny and she looked exactly like you, Lieutenant. She had the same blonde hair; the same hair-style; the same eyes; the same shape, and even the same voice. I could stand the two of you side by side and your own mothers wouldn't know which was which.' He drew a sharp breath and added flatly, 'And she was a tramp. She was the bitchiest little tramp that ever walked.'

Rona had nothing to say, but after a moment Canning went on. 'I'm sorry, Lieutenant, but you were just standing in for your double. It took me a long while to realise that the similarity was only in appearance; that beauty was only skin deep.'

Rona breathed slowly and then relaxed again. 'Why was she a tramp?'

Canning told her everything about the incident at the Kensington flat. There seemed no point in stopping half-way and after the way he had treated her he felt that she had a right to know. He kept his voice level despite the underlying tone of bitter anger and he finished by saying harshly:

'She was too damned lazy to step down from her own fancy world and get herself a proper job — she preferred to sell herself to Mister-bloody-Harvey in return for a few more modelling dates.'

When he stopped Rona said bluntly:

'All right, so she was a tramp. And you feel bloody sorry for yourself. But do you really believe that it's always that way about? That it's always the man who gets let down?'

Canning stared at her, but words failed him.

'I couldn't help it if I just happened to look like your ex-girl-friend, but maybe I was a little bit to blame for that hostile atmosphere we created between us. I had damned good reasons for staying apart from the common soldiery and acting my rank all the time.' She paused for breath and blazed on, 'When I was first commissioned I was fool enough to get emotionally involved with a young private in an army hospital. It's the one mistake we're not supposed to make and I'd been warned about it a thousand times — but I thought this time was different. But it wasn't different. He boasted of his so-called conquest, and I was saddled with a dirty reputation. I was eventually transferred to another unit. Since then I've kept my distance from temptation.'

There was another awkward silence, and then she started to turn away. But Canning stopped her.

He said 'Lieutenant Waring I still owe you a proper apology.'

She turned back to him and shook her head:

'That wasn't what I wanted. I just

wanted to clear the air. The strain of sitting in solid silence in that blasted cab was driving me slowly insane. It was worse than waiting for the Bantu to attack.'

Canning groped for something else to say. The Kangzi swirled softly behind him and the blanket of rustling jungle cut them apart from the rest of the world. Rona looked at him hesitantly and then turned away for the second time.

Canning reached out and fastened his free hand on her shoulder. She seemed to tremble in mid-movement and then turned her head to look at him again her eyes were expectant yet unsure. Canning moved closer and turned her round to face him their bodies were almost touching.

He said quietly 'I'm not the boasting kind Lieutenant. I may be the most sullen, insolent, downright surly example of a soldier that you've ever met — but I don't brag.'

He pulled her gently close, his right arm encircling her waist. He still held the sten gun in his left hand and he held her against him with one arm as his mouth slowly merged against her cracked lips. She was stiff but the stiffness melted out of her as her eyes closed and she accepted his kiss.

He drew his face away and said softly:

'That just means that we've properly buried the hatchet. It won't happen again.'

'But I want it to happen again.' She plucked the sten gun from his fingers and let it fall gently to the grassy earth. Her arms moved round his shoulders and she said equally softly, 'Please kiss me again, Corporal — that's an order.'

Prisoner of the Bantu

The first light of dawn filtered greyly through the darkness beyond the Kangzi, the sweeping curve of the river became more distinct and the silhouettes of tree and jungle emerged more sharply out of the night. A feeble grey light dared to invade the gloom and broken swirls of water became visible where the Congo river tumbled over a half-submerged sandbank in mid-stream. At any moment the sun would burst above the eastern horizon and already the first flush of pale pink had infiltrated the charcoal-grey of the sky.

Rona Waring sat wide-awake in the cab of the ambulance with the sten gun lying close against her right thigh. She had been keeping watch for the past two hours while Canning slept and now she experienced a faint tingle of misgiving as she watched the gradual advance of daylight. She wondered whether the end of the new day would find them some place of safety, or whether fresh disaster was awaiting the ill-fated ambulance under the searing African sun.

She glanced slowly at Canning on the opposite side of the cab, the Corporal's eyes were closed and his chin rested on his chest as he slumped back in the corner, but even in sleep the stubborn lines showed clearly in his strong-boned face. His arms were folded and he was breathing softly through the nose, his mouth was closed in a firm, unyielding line. Rona smiled as her scrutiny reached his mouth. The mouth was deceptive, for the hard, sullen lips had been surprisingly gentle as they caressed her own.

She thought back to the previous night and wondered whether she was making a fool of herself for the second time, but in their present situation the question lacked importance. She had stopped thinking as an officer soon after Canning had slapped her out of her single spate of hysterics, and she was secretly glad that the Corporal has assumed command. It had hurt to be virtually stripped of her rank, but basically she knew that he had been right. The job of getting the ambulance with its suffering cargo of wounded men to safety called for a man at the wheel, and Corporal David Canning was undoubtedly the right man for the job.

He had instructed her to shake him as soon as it was light enough to drive on, but she had to make the round of her patients first and she saw no reason to wake him until the last moment. The cab door on her side was already ajar and she pushed it silently open and stepped down on to the grass. She went to the back of the ambulance and opened the doors.

Baxter relaxed and allowed his hand to fall away from his sten as she entered. He lay on his back looking up at her and forced a faint smile on to his greying face. The others were all asleep.

Rona knelt and peeled back the torn shreds of the tall man's trouser leg and winced at the bloody mess of bandages that shrouded his foot and ankle. There was nothing she could do by interfering with the bandages and it was kindest to leave them alone. She looked into Baxter's face and asked softly:

'How does it feel?'

Baxter said dully, 'It's bloody murder. I'll be glad when they cut it off.'

Rona felt empty inside. She had tried to hide the fact that the shattered bones were beyond repair and that the foot would eventually have to be amputated, and she wondered how long it was since Baxter had realised the truth. Now she found she couldn't lie to him and said slowly:

'It won't be long now. Even by going the long way round we should reach Ningini by tonight, and then we'll have a helicopter to fly you straight out to hospital.' Her tone became less certain as she finished, for she remembered promising them helicopters and hospitals when they reached Sakinda, and they had passed Sakinda a long, long time ago.

Baxter said nothing and at last she turned to attend to the others. Hardman was in bad shape, but no worse than yesterday, he was asleep and she did not wake him. Delayney opened his eyes as she leaned over his bed, but he said nothing. She realised that Delayney was also suffering badly, and guessed that he had got very little sleep during the night.

She straightened up to look at Garner on the top bed and received the first encouraging sign of the day. Garner's eyes were open and he was obviously through the worst of whatever jungle fever had struck him down. His face was waxen under the stubble that covered his chin and he looked terribly weak.

Rona said gently, 'It's about time you woke up. How do you feel?'

Garner stared at her, his eyes were very dark and glazed and he seemed unable to focus properly on her face. Then his lips moved and framed the single word, 'water.'

Rona hesitated, and then picked up the bottle that Canning had filled from the river and trickled a few drops of the sour-looking liquid into the man's mouth. Garner swallowed painfully and then closed his eyes. Rona watched him for a minute and then decided that

Garner would live, he only needed rest and nourishment to build up his fever-weakened body. She straightened his pillow to make him more comfortable and then turned her attention to Morris.

The little man had been sleeping on the floor with his good shoulder propped against the three remaining petrol cans, but now he was fully awake and watching her. She gave him a smile and knelt to examine his arm and straighten the sling. There was a kind of stringy toughness in the little gingerhaired man and he bore it stolidly. When she had finished he asked her to help him to his feet, to 'go water the daisies,' as he vaguely phrased it.

Morris was quite capable once on his feet and she left him to it and returned to the cab. Canning still slept and she wondered whether she dared awaken him with a kiss. She decided against it and shook him gently instead.

Canning was awake immediately. He looked up at her and yawned.

'Good morning, Lieutenant. Are you fit?'

The word Lieutenant sounded strangely

hesitant on his lips after he had tenderly called her Rona only a few hours before, and she wondered whether Corporal was going to sound just as awkward after she had called him David. She decided to try it.

'Fit enough, Corporal. Apart from being starving hungry, gloriously filthy, and probably the most unappetising woman you've ever clapped eyes on, I think I can loosely describe myself as being fit.'

Canning smiled as he straightened up and automatically reached for the sten gun. 'I can't do anything about the starving hungry bit for the moment,' he said wryly. 'But the glorious filth should wash off, even though the bathroom is a bit primitive. You've got the time while I top up the petrol tank and take a quick look at the lads, but for Pete's sake don't stray too far or finish up as breakfast for a hungry crocodile. I should hate to lose you at this stage.'

'I've already made the men as comfortable as possible,' Rona smiled. 'But I'll still take five minutes while you're topping up the tank. I haven't washed for two whole days, and although that ripe, sweaty tang may smell nice and masculine on you, it's not exactly becoming on a lady.'

Canning raised his eyebrows in faint wonderment as past thoughts flickered from his memory, and decided that Rona Waring was becoming less and less like Jenny with every passing moment.

They climbed down from the cab and Canning unscrewed the cap on the petrol tank and squinted inside. He had poured in two gallons from the second can during the return journey to Sakinda and now there was room for the rest of the can below the level of the jagged hole. Rona watched him and then turned towards the Kangzi.

Canning said, 'You'd better take the sten.'

She shook her head and smiled, 'I'd rather not. Then if anything horrible invades my bathroom I can scream for you.'

She carried on towards the river and Canning watched her go. He decided that she was sensible enough to take care of herself and then switched his attention to the job of topping up the tank.

Rona reached the river bank and then turned upstream away from the ambulance. The curtain of jungle soon shut the scarred red crosses on its steel sides from view and she stopped where the river washed through a miniature cove of hard-packed mud. There were faint impressions of webbed feet, bird claws and tiny hooves at the water's edge, but for the moment the grey mud was devoid of life. On the far side of the river a flight of herons swept upwards in a graceful V formation where the rising sun was already turning the Kangzi from metallic grey to a rich wine red. A kingfisher darted over the cove in a flash of brilliant colour and the sunrise was now well-established in a blazing sea of scarlet and orange ripples across the eastern sky. The tangled foliage around her was green and dew fresh, and splashed with occasional flames of tropical flower. Africa was showing her sweetest face, but Rona was not fooled and she looked around warily for crocodiles before nearing the water.

There were no scaly monsters in sight and she stepped quickly to the water's edge. She could hear the birds and monkeys kicking up their normal din of excited chatter but there was no hint of anything more threatening in the vicinity. She pulled off her blouse and dipped her arms into the shallow water, breathing a luxurious sigh of pleasure as the engrained dust was swilled away from her skin.

She didn't see Morris as he wandered back along the river bank. The little man had slept very little during the night due to the angry throbbing of his arm and the perpetual headache that accompanied the glancing wound across his temple, and he had been glad of the chance to get out of the cramped confines of the ambulance for a few moments. When Rona had left him to wake Canning he had taken the opportunity to rove farther afield than was strictly necessary in order to stretch his legs, and now he unexpectedly found her between himself and the ambulance.

Morris had been moving quietly, looking around him with the wondering eyes of a city man whose normal conception of the countryside was a mental picture of Hyde Park, and Rona did not hear him approach. Morris stopped, half hidden by a tangle of bushes and unsure whether to hurry past or turn back and then advance more noisily. As he watched Rona straightened her back and twisted her arms behind her to reach the snap of her bra between her shoulder blades. The black lace slipped away in her hand and for a moment her proud-nippled breasts were thrust forward in classic profile before she bent forwards to wash the upper half of her body. Despite himself Morris was unable to tear his eyes away.

The cool water was like a balm to her sweat-stained skin and suddenly Rona straightened up and glanced around her. She needed a proper bath more than anything else and there still wasn't a crocodile in sight. The Kangzi looked reasonably clear at this point and she argued that a thirty second dip couldn't possibly put her in any danger. On sudden impulse she unzipped her skirt before she changed her mind.

Morris crouched lower behind the concealing bushes and was suddenly afraid that if he did try to retreat now she could not possibly fail to hear him. He didn't want her to catch him spying, and he didn't want her to think that he had intended to spy, but for the moment he was rooted to the spot. He had the crazy feeling that at least he ought to close his eyes, but his eyes remained open just the same. He watched her peel off her stockings and the flimsy black panties that matched the bra and his heart thumped painfully in his chest. The smooth, naked lines of her figure were unbelievably exciting now that she had stripped away the nurse's uniform, and the sight of the unexpectedly proud breasts made him swallow hard.

Rona waded out into the Kangzi and dived forwards, revelling in the cold shock as the water closed over her body. She came up, kicked forward a few glorifying strokes and then swam back to waist-deep water. Swiftly she rubbed the remaining traces of sweat and dirt from her limbs and then hurried back towards her clothes. The one quick immersion was all the time she dared spare, and she still remembered Canning's warning about crocodiles.

She picked up her blouse and used it to dry most of the dampness from her body, towelling swiftly as she rubbed her hips and thighs. She climbed into her panties and zipped up her skirt, dressing fast because by now Canning was probably waiting for her to return. For a moment she frowned at the wet blouse in her hand, and then she knelt to give it a quick wash.

She didn't see the movement in the bushes behind her, and she didn't hear the stealthy parting of the branches. Seven Bantu warriors emerged from the tangled jungle like tip-toeing demons entering the scene of some fantastic stage setting. They wore nothing but soiled loin-cloths and each man carried a brand new automatic rifle. They stared at the kneeling girl and slowly their negroid faces became affected with simple, child-like grins.

Rona Waring felt their presence as though some weird and invisible force had reached silently to touch her mind. She froze in the act of wringing the water from her blouse and felt as though her bowels had suddenly melted into iced water. She sensed the watching eyes upon her naked back, and when she slowly forced herself to turn she knew exactly what she would find.

Fear gripped her as she stared up at the silently grinning natives, and she swallowed back the aching desire to scream.

She was less than fifty yards from the ambulance which was completely screened by jungle and if she screamed she knew that Canning would come running with his sten. And if Canning came running he would run to his death for he would be no match for seven well-armed warriors on their own ground. She knew she must not bring Canning to his death for that would lead to the discovery of the ambulance and the end for all of them.

She straightened up and slowly donned her wet blouse. The leader of the Bantu chuckled and moved forward and she made no sound as they hustled her away. She was praying silently that Canning would do nothing stupid like trying to find her, but would drive on with the wounded men the moment he realised that something was wrong.

One Man's Secret

Canning had topped up the ambulance's petrol tank as much as he was able and then slung the second empty can into the undergrowth. He picked up his sten and moved into the back of the half-hidden vehicle to talk to Hardman while he waited for Rona to return. The big Sergeant was now awake and talking feebly, and Canning wondered again what kind of spark kept the man alive when he should have long ago been dead. He had noticed that Morris was missing but a word from Delayney had explained the little man's absence.

The five-minute time limit that Rona had set herself was up, but Canning barely gave it a thought. He remembered the luxury of washing the thick dust from his own face and arms the night before and he did not begrudge her a few extra minutes. He did not even look up when he heard Morris scrambling back through the entangling vegetation.

Morris did not dare call out and his heart was thumping with sickly speed as he stumbled towards the ambulance. He almost fell and the crackling of branch and grasses beneath his feet sounded horribly loud as the comforting sight of the big red cross on the white ground came into view. He pulled himself panting into the ambulance and almost choked with relief when he saw Canning sitting on the edge of Hardman's bed.

'Corp!' he blurted urgently, controlling his voice almost to a whisper.

Canning looked up, 'What is it?'

'It's the Lieutenant.' Morris was still struggling for breath and his arm was throbbing so furiously where he had knocked it during his frantic rush to the ambulance that he could hardly speak. 'I was watching her take her swim and — and — ' He broke off in staring alarm as he saw the look that appeared in Canning's grey eyes, and the rest of what he had to say got stuck in his throat.

Canning said savagely, 'You bloody little Peeping Tom.'

313

He ignored a sudden yelp of pain from Baxter as his foot kicked against the sick man's pillow and he lunged angrily towards Morris. He caught hold of the little man's shirt and twisted violently.

'You bloody Peeping Tom,' he said again. 'After all she's done for you you still have to sneak off and spy on her.'

'No, Corp. It wasn't like that.' Morris twisted frantically as his frightened eyes searched for help. 'Sergeant Hardman!' he gasped. 'Irish!'

Delayney was already struggling round on his bed, the lower half of his body was crippled but there was still strength in his shoulders and he grabbed Canning's arm with both hands.

'Let go of him,' he gritted. 'He's my mate and nobody's knocking him about. He's got a bad arm.'

For a second Canning struggled with the two of them, and then Hardman ordered weakly:

'Let him go, Corporal. He didn't come straight here just to confess that he's been peeping. There's more to it.'

Canning realised abruptly that Hardman

314

was right, and sick fear rushed in to replace the anger that drained swiftly from his heart. He shook Delayney away but still held on to Morris's shirt-front as he demanded fiercely:

'What's happened? Where is she?'

Morris said hoarsely, 'I wasn't peeping, Corp. Not deliberately. Honest.'

But Canning had realised now that something was desperately wrong and he no longer cared whether Morris had been deliberately peeping or not. He shook the little man in exasperation and snapped again:

'For Christ's sake — what's happened?'

'It — it was the wogs. Seven or eight of them. They just walked up and took her. There was nothing — '

Morris's recital ended in a gasp of pain as Canning pushed him aside and snatched up his sten. The little man backed away hugging his injured arm but the Corporal was already crashing away through the undergrowth with the sten in his hands.

Canning ran with cold dread in his heart, heedless of the noise he made as he knocked ferns and branches out of his path. He reached the river and raced upstream, covering the ground in great leaping strides — and then he reached the empty cove where Rona had bathed, and stopped dead.

He could see her footprints blurring the traces of birds and antelope that had drank at the water's edge before the sun was up. And beside them lay the nylon stockings she had not bothered to put on again because the brush had laddered them so badly; and the black lace bra that the Bantu had forced her to leave behind as well. There was nothing else.

He stared into the tangled wall of greenery all around, and he couldn't even find one broken branch to mark the way they had taken her. The sten was a useless lump of metal in his hands and he had never felt so helpless in his life. Why hadn't she shouted, he wondered dully. If only she had shouted he could have been with her in a matter of seconds.

He walked out on to the hard-packed grey mud and stared down at the ruined stockings and the twin cups of black lace.

It just didn't seem possible that this was all that was left.

After a few minutes he straightened up and again stared at the wall of jungle. It was hopeless to try and follow them into that for he had not the faintest idea of which direction they had taken. At the moment he made a perfectly clear target as he stood with his back to the Kangzi and he realised that if the Bantu were still within hearing they would probably have taken a shot at him by now. They had melted completely away into the jungle and taken Rona Waring with them.

He wondered whether they had been afraid to attack the ambulance, or whether they had simply not realised that it was so close by; but the answer did not really seem to matter. The Congolese terrorists were no strangers to rape and worse, and even grey-haired nuns received no mercy. The thoughts of Rona in their hands were twisting barbs of hell in Canning's brain.

Why in heaven's name had she submitted so tamely without resistance? She knew that he was only seconds away!

He still stared at the unanswering jungle and tried desperately to reason out what the next move of the tribesmen might be. Would they rape her and slit her throat, or would they take her back to Sakinda first? The last possibility gave Canning a flickering hope, for if the natives were from Sakinda then there was a strong chance that they would take her back to Larocque. The mercenary had his own unknown reasons for wanting the ambulance stopped and it was almost certain that he would have given orders for any captives to be brought back to the village.

Canning did not hesitate any longer but returned grimfaced to the ambulance. He knew that there wasn't the ghost of a chance of finding her in the jungle, and even if there was her captors would hear him coming long before he heard them and simply lay in ambush — but he had already made up his mind what to do.

Baxter and Delayney were waiting with their stens cocked when he climbed into the ambulance again. Morris stood at the back still tentatively holding his injured arm. The little man said helplessly:

'I'm sorry, Corp. I couldn't do nothing. If I'd had a gun — or if I just had two hands — '

Canning knew that Morris was right, the little man had aided Rona once but this time there had been absolutely nothing he could do except stand by and watch. He said grimly:

'It's not your fault. I'm not blaming anyone.'

'Then there's no trace of her?' It was Hardman who spoke.

'No.' Canning found that his voice was bluntly calm and betrayed no hint of his feelings. He went on, 'They've just vanished into the jungle, but if they were part of our friend Larocque's band of merry butchers then they've almost certainly taken her back to Sakinda. And I'm going into Sakinda to fetch her out again before we drive on.'

Delayney gave him a hard stare. 'You're mad, Corp. How the hell can you pull off a one man cavalry charge?'

Canning said flatly, 'I wasn't thinking

of a one man cavalry charge — just a straight swap.'

An uncomprehending silence greeted him, and then Hardman roused himself weakly on to one elbow and said:

'What's on your mind, Corporal? What do you mean by a straight swap?'

Canning looked slowly around the faces of the four men, and his grey eyes were hard and unblinking. Baxter had relaxed and allowed his sten to fall back to the floor and the Corporal's foot rested upon it almost as though the move was accidental. In the same moment the sten in his hands angled towards Delayney and firmly pressed the Irishman's gun flat against the pillow.

He said softly, 'Larocque doesn't want Lieutenant Waring — he wants one of you men. He either wants one of you personally, or he wants something or some information that one of you is carrying. And I want to know which one of you he's after. That's what I mean by a swap.'

His gaze searched each face in turn. Hardman and Baxter were both looking sick and pale, and he had to remind himself that they were both sick men and suffering a lot of pain. Morris's shrimp-like face was damp with sweat, but Morris had been sweating hard when he brought the news of Rona's capture. Delayney looked undecided about pulling his sten gun free and calling his bluff, but not quite aggressive enough to take the risk.

Hardman said uncertainly, 'You really mean to hand one of us over to Larocque?'

'That's right, Sarge.' Canning's voice was about thirty degrees below zero. 'It's just a matter of simple exchange. One yellow-gutted bastard who's been the cause of all our troubles anyway, for one white woman who's worth more than the bloody lot of you put together. I don't call that exchange any robbery.'

There was another slow, staring silence as he looked from one to the other, and then his gaze rested on Hardman again.

'Are you the man who Larocque is after, Sarge?'

Hardman's eyes were as unflinching as

Canning's own. He said flatly and very distinctly:

'I can't think of any reason why I should be, Corporal. No reason at all.'

Canning held the sick man's gaze for almost a minute, and then he nodded slowly and turned back to the other three.

'I seem to remember asking you lads before,' he said softly. 'But this time I want an answer.' He stared at Morris.

The little man shook his head. 'No, Corp. It ain't me. I don't know anything.'

Delayney said harshly, 'Leave him alone, Corp. He doesn't know a damn thing. We're mates, and if he knew anything I'd know it too.'

Canning lifted his sten slowly so that instead of pinning the Irishman's gun to the bed it was pointing directly at his face.

'And what do you know, Delayney? Anything?'

'I know sweet Fanny All!'

'And I suppose ginger-top here is your alibi in turn, because you're both mates. You hold each other's hands every time you go out in the dark.'

'That's right.' Delayney's voice had it's own note of menace now.

Canning smiled but his voice had frozen by another degree. He said, 'So that only means that you're either both innocent — or both guilty. Doesn't it?'

Delayney's lips tightened and he glared belligerently. Canning held the stare for longer than he had held Hardman's, and then he turned his unrelenting eyes towards Baxter.

The tall man smiled thinly and shook his head.

'The answer is still no, Corp.'

Canning's eyes ached and he was boiling with frustration, and then suddenly he remembered the top bed. His earlier suspicions flooded back and he moved closer to look into the fever-ravaged face of Private Garner. Garner's eyes were open but he was staring blankly up at the roof and his body was completely motionless.

Canning ripped the covering away from the sick man and grabbed him savagely by the shoulder, pulling him violently on to one side so that they were face to face.

'What about you, chum?' He almost spat the words out. 'What do you know about a man named Larocque?'

Garner's eyes slowly lost their glazed look and his mouth gaped helplessly. He blinked and then worked his lips and throat with slow, excruciating effort.

'Water,' he mumbled vaguely. 'Water.'

'Larocque!' Canning insisted. 'What do you know of Larocque?'

He shook the man in blind fury and then Hardman said sharply:

'Stop that, Corporal. Garner can't be the man you want.'

Canning turned his head, slowly, and unbelievably.

Then Hardman went on, 'You told us that Larocque saw the man he wanted at the stream where we were first ambushed, so it couldn't possibly have been Garner. Garner was half-dead with fever and hidden in the ambulance all the time. It must have been someone who was in the action. It has to be one of us.'

Canning knew that Hardman had to be right, and gently he lowered Garner back to his bed and pulled the blankets straight. Then he said:

'All right, so it has to be one of you: Baxter, Hardman, Delayney or Morris. Which is it?'

Baxter said slowly, 'What about the two men you buried, Foster and your own mate? It could have been one of them.'

Canning hesitated, and then said grimly, 'I don't believe it could possibly have been Roy Spencer — I knew him too well. That leaves Foster as a possibility but the odds are four to one against — and I'm betting that the man I want is still here.'

No one answered him, and their faces told him nothing. The air was strangely hushed and for the moment even the birds had stopped their noisy chattering outside. Canning mentally ticked off their names again as he looked round the shadowed interior of the ambulance; Delayney, Morris, Baxter, Hardman. It had to be one of them. But not one pair of eyes flinched away from his searching gaze.

A minute passed — two minutes — and still no one answered. The unnatural hush persisted, enveloping them in a gradually thickening cloak of high-pressured silence. Morris swallowed suddenly, his larynx jerking in a convulsive gulping movement. Delayney was watchful, wary. A nerve twitched once at the corner of Baxter's mouth.

Canning felt the blind frustration that had gripped him slowly harden into something solid, and he knew exactly what he was going to do. He lifted his sten once more to cover Delayney, holding it in one hand with the butt tucked under his arm, with his free hand he picked up the Irishman's gun from the bed. Delayney watched as his precious sten gun was tossed into the undergrowth outside the ambulance, but still he said nothing. Canning turned his own sten on to Baxter and stepped quietly back. Baxter's sten gun followed Delayney's into the jungle.

Canning smiled and said softly, 'I've just thought of the perfect answer. I'll drive the bloody lot of you back to

Sakinda and let friend Larocque take his pick.' Then he turned and jumped briskly down from the ambulance, reaching out to slam shut the first of the double rear doors.

'Wait, Corp!'

Canning stopped in mid-movement, and then turned back slowly.

Baxter was fishing into the top pocket of his shirt, but there was still no expression on his face. He pulled out a folded square of paper and said flatly:

'I think this could be what you want.'

Canning took the paper from Baxter's out-stretched hand, but his eyes never left the tall man's face.

'What is it?'

Baxter said, 'If a drunken down-and-out named Contin was telling anything near the truth it's a map. Katanga stinks of copper — that's what the nigger politicians are tearing each other's eyes out for, and why we're here to try and keep the bloody peace — but if Contin was right then the vein located on that map could open up the richest mine yet.'

Canning's eyes were bleak and decidedly ugly. He said:

'Go on.'

The nerve twitched for the second time at the corner of Baxter's mouth, but he continued in the same flat tone.

'Contin was sick-scared and full of brandy when I found him in a bar in Leopoldville, and he had just spent his last handful of Belgian francs on the bottle. He'd double-crossed his partner to steal that map, but somehow he'd messed up the job and the partner was still alive and looking for him. He said that the copper vein marked on that map would be worth a small fortune to whoever came out on top in the struggle for Katanga, but he couldn't get near enough to any of the dark boys pulling the strings to try and do a deal. When I came on the scene he was somewhere between a nervous breakdown and stark raving mad. He was desperate to get out of the Congo and willing to trade with anyone who'd give him the price of a plane ticket. I picked him up when he fell out of his chair and I guess he just

328

had to spill his guts to someone. He spilled them to me and wound up by begging me to buy his precious map.'

'So you bought it?' Canning's voice was hard.

Baxter shook his head, 'No, Corp. For one thing I thought it was all a cock-and-bull story, and for another I hadn't got the price of a plane ticket either. But eventually Contin passed out and I helped the bar-tender to lug him upstairs out of the way. The bar-tender went back to his bar and I just looked at Contin and thought for a bit. The yarn Contin had told me might have been a drunken fairy story to con a gullible soldier out of some of his hard-earned pay — but on the other hand there's so much murder, raping and back-stabbing going on in the Congo that it just might be true. And if it was true then the location of a fortune was crumpled up in Contin's dirty pocket. Maybe I didn't know how to cash in on it, but neither did Contin. I figured that I had nothing to lose, transferred the map from his pocket to my own, and then left him.'

'And?'

'And nothing. For the moment there was nothing that I could do with the map so I just forgot it. But Contin said that the partner he double-crossed was looking for him, and it's possible that the partner eventually caught up with him. And the partner could be Larocque.'

'And Contin gave Larocque your description.'

Baxter grinned wryly. 'He was probably able to give Larocque my name, rank, number and blasted photograph. I missed my wallet when I got back to camp, and I'm damned sure that I heard something fall when I was lugging Contin up those narrow stairs. There was nothing in it but a couple of letters, my own picture, and a handful of near worthless Congo notes that were losing value every minute, so I didn't bother to go back. I couldn't visualise Contin rushing off to the police with it, and I hadn't got the time anyway.'

There was a moment of silence and then Canning said grimly, 'So now we know. I'll drive the ambulance back as far as the fork and then walk into Sakinda. I'll tell Larocque that he can have his map back in return for Rona Waring.'

Hardman roused himself weakly, his lips tightening as the movement stretched the bloodied bandages across his chest:

'Don't rush things, Corporal. Think first. Larocque will probably make the exchange if you can get to him, but you've got to reach him first. The blacks will most likely butcher you as soon as you show your face in the village.'

Canning said slowly, 'It's a risk, but it's been done before. It was only a couple of weeks ago that an army Major strolled into one of these Congo villages with a swagger stick under his arm and brought out a party of priests to a waiting helicopter. The natives have a simple mentality, and if they see anything unusual their first reaction is to stand and stare. I think that if I walk into Sakinda unarmed and try not to look too much like I'll feel, I'll probably get away with it. They won't be all worked up for a fight at this time of morning, and I only want them to forget about their trigger fingers and gawp for a couple of moments while I walk across to Larocque's hut. Then I can claim his protection.'

The thought of relying on the mercenary for protection brought a bitter tightening of cold knots to Canning's stomach, and nobody had any more comments to make.

The Gamble That Failed

The last mile back to Sakinda was the longest mile that Canning ever walked. He had waited for three agonising hours to give the Bantu time to hustle Rona Waring back to the village, praying all the while that they were taking her back to Larocque and not brutally raping her in the jungle while he was powerless to stop them. Finally he had climbed into his cab and driven the ambulance back to the fork in the road, turning it to face the Kangzi again and then backing it into the edge of the jungle out of sight. He knew that there was a strong chance that he would not be coming back and he grimly helped Morris into the driving seat. The little man could drive with one hand but he needed someone beside him to manoeuvre the gear stick. Delayney volunteered first, but Canning doubted whether the Irishman could sit upright with his weight on his injured thigh

333

without passing out, and so he had chosen Baxter. The tall man gritted his teeth as Canning helped him round to the cab, but once he was sitting inside with his shattered foot again supported by pillows he confirmed hoarsely that he was capable of doing what was necessary. Canning gave him back his sten and then returned the second sten to Delayney. He told them to give him three more hours and if he was not back by then to drive on without him. Then he had started to walk back to Sakinda.

There were a lot of doubts in Canning's mind as he walked back down the jungle-flanked dirt track of the Congo road. The odds were stacked heavily against him for the Bantu tribesmen might easily hack him to pieces on impulse before he could get to Larocque, and even if he reached the mercenary the man might not be willing, or even able, to make the trade, for there was no way of knowing how much control he really had over his black allies. And above all was the sick, heart-chilling fear that Rona might already be lying dead in some dank forest glade, her naked body violated and butchered before being left for the hyenas and vultures, and other grisly scavengers of the jungle.

It was strange to be walking empty-handed, without the comforting presence of the sten gun. But Canning knew that the sight of the sten could easily goad some excitable black into spearing him before they realised that he did not mean to use it, and so he had left the sten with Hardman. There was not much that the big Sergeant could do with it if the half-concealed ambulance were to be discovered, but even while helpless on his back he could point it in the general direction of the open doors and pull the trigger. It would merely be a token resistance, but Canning knew that Hardman would die happier with even the most feeble attempt at a fight.

The sun was as hot as it had ever been, but for once Canning was hardly aware of the heat as he walked down the centre of the road. He saw no reason for skulking along the edge of the jungle for if he encountered any of the Bantu before reaching the village he wanted to do nothing to alarm them. His arms swung loosely at his sides and without being consciously aware of it he had adopted the stride and pace of a soldier on the march. He thought again of the swagger-stick Major who had taken a similar stroll into a terrorist village to demand the release of white captives, and he hoped that the Bantu had as much respect for a Corporal's stripes as they had for the epaulets of a Major.

Every yard of the road gave him the feeling that he was walking a tightrope into hell, but his stride refused to falter as he pushed stolidly on. He didn't even look at the jungle barrier on either side but kept his eyes straight ahead. His mouth had dried up once more and his shirt was plastered to his back with sweat. His heavy army boots puffed up a small cloud of powdery dust each time they descended with flat regularity on the road.

At last he walked into Sakinda. The barrier of forest jungle simply ended on each side and he was only sixty yards from the village compound. Over on his left was the grass plain that Rona had fired two nights ago, now a black wasteland that swept up to the edge of the village and then veered away to the south. It was the only sign of the fire's passing for now the stampeded cattle had been rounded up and returned to the hastily rebuilt kraals. Some of the mud and wattle huts had been reconstructed and the sky above was a peaceful but agonisingly bright blue. The only twists of smoke that now marred the blueness came from the wood cooking fires that still burned here and there. As Canning had expected the village had been re-occupied by Larocque's Bantu, and the open spaces between the huts were an idle sea of lazing black warriors.

Canning walked slowly across the last sixty yards. The bubble of aimless chatter suddenly faltered as the nearer natives became aware of his approach. A hundred black hands reached instinctively for spears or rifles, hesitated, and then stayed. Canning swallowed hard as a hundred pairs of wondering eyes became

337

rooted on his face and killed the sudden frightening compulsion to turn and run. If he ran now his back would become a bloody sponge, soaking up a solid hail of lead and spear blades.

He had to pass directly under the three great trees as he entered the compound and he noted with a swamping feeling of relief that the bodies of Sergeant Riley and his men had at last been cut down. He had had the ghastly premonition that a single drip of blood from one of the corpses as he passed underneath would have been all that was needed to stir the Bantu into fresh butchery. Just one taste of blood could snap them abruptly from their staring hesitancy and incite them into a new lust for murder.

The silence had spread now as one by one more of the negro faces had swivelled round to gape as he walked steadily towards them. Those at the back had straightened warily to their feet to see over the heads of their companions, their weapons resting lightly in their hands. The nearest warriors squatted only yards away, doubt and irresolution registering in their widened eyes. A spear lifted, wavered, and then dropped again. Canning's shoulders prickled with expectancy as he walked past and Larocque's hut looked to be a thousand miles away through the black horde.

Suddenly a new fear knifed through Canning's heart, causing him to falter and almost stop in mid-stride. He had assumed all along that Larocque would still be in his hut, but suppose the mercenary had left the village! Larocque might well have left in an effort to track down the missing ambulance, and the hut that should spell safety might well be empty.

Despite himself Canning walked on, knowing that it was too late to turn back now. Any sign of receding determination on his part could supply the necessary signal to unleash the spears and the war cries. And he knew that all they needed was a signal.

He crossed the compound and the first of the black ranks separated slowly to let him through. There was an absolute hush blanketing the village now and almost two hundred pairs of eyes followed his calm, measured progress. The way ahead was blocked by waiting warriors but one by one they stepped aside. And then, as was inevitable, he reached the warrior who stood his ground.

The man wore an ancient pair of tattered shorts and an old open shirt that was knotted about his middle, but he was barefoot and held a large-bladed spear in both hands. The thick negroid lips were pursed in a doubtful scowl but his eyes lacked the same high degree of perplexity as those of his companions. He was slender and muscular, and he was young — dangerously young, for youth craved glory, and blood and glory went hand in hand.

The young Bantu stood squarely in Canning's path and the advancing Corporal knew that if he changed course to avoid the issue then he was lost. Their eyes met and Canning knew that he had to out-stare his enemy. They were only a dozen paces apart and the whole village tensed in expectation as they awaited the outcome.

340

Canning did not falter and slowly the young Bantu's spear swung up to level upon the Corporal's stomach. Canning did not take his eyes from the Bantu's face.

Five paces separated them . . . four . . . three . . . and then on the third deliberately unhurried pace Canning swung his arm to knock the menacing spear brusquely aside. The warrior hesitated and then his gaze flinched away. He stepped to one side and Canning moved past him with his eyes still fixed directly ahead.

There was a movement in the doorway of Larocque's hut, and then suddenly the mercenary emerged from the gloom and straightened his back. He stared at the approaching Canning and for a moment he actually blinked. The hush of silence became less oppressive and Canning realised that he was over the first agonising hurdle. He had reached Larocque.

Larocque was still wearing a bush shirt and shorts, but for the moment he was unarmed. His lean, darkly-bronzed face

341

was wrinkled with surprise, but slowly the dark features smoothed and he smiled. He folded his arms to strike an arrogant pose that was mostly for the benefit of his gaping allies and waited.

Canning covered the last few yards and stopped only a few feet away. He was several inches shorter than the tall Belgian, but his grey eyes were still hard and steady when their gaze met. He waited in silence and his stubborn streak determined that Larocque would have to speak first.

The mercenary said at last, 'You must be the driver of that damned ambulance. You'd better come inside.'

He turned and ducked his head to re-enter the hut, and Canning followed.

There was no light in the large hut and for a moment Canning could distinguish nothing in the darkened gloom. Then a gasping, unbelieving utterance of his own name jerked his attention to the far reaches of the hut. Relief thawed his heart in a torrential flood of released emotion as he recognised the voice of Rona Waring and he plunged eagerly

342

forward. The agonising jab of a rifle barrel low in the stomach brought him to an abrupt, jack-knifing halt, and his heart froze again as he recognised the old negro Mambiro at the other end of the rifle.

There was a moment of silence as his eyes became accustomed to the darkness, and slowly he made out the sprawling outline of the nurse lying full length on the hard-packed dirt of the floor behind the Bantu chieftain. She was lying on one shoulder with her head raised to stare at him with dulled, hopeless eyes, and there was a livid weal across the right side of her face. Her buttonless blouse had again sagged open but this time she was unable to pull the edges together for her hands were tied behind her back.

She said wretchedly, 'Dear David, why did you come? You can't do anything.'

Larocque said calmly, 'That's a good question, Corporal. Why did you come?'

Canning didn't answer. The rifle was still only inches from his stomach and he couldn't take his eyes away from Mambiro's face. The old negro's features were evilly wrinkled and his eyes held a sharp, piercing glitter. His thick lips were peeled back to half-bare his teeth and he seemed to be hovering on the very edge of pulling the trigger. Canning swallowed hard and felt the sweat grow colder on his back.

Larocque moved closer to lay a restraining hand on the rifle:

'Wait, Mambiro. Let him talk.'

The old negro was unmoved. He said harshly:

'He should die. Katanga is black man's country now; the greedy white filth should go back to their own lands. We don't want interference. We don't want United Nations. We don't want anything white. They must learn that Katanga belongs to the black man.'

Larocque nodded sagely, 'That is so — but we can listen to him talk.'

Mambiro pouted his thick lips and abruptly jerked the rifle away. He scowled at Larocque but said nothing. Canning breathed again.

Larocque said evenly, 'Let's start again. Why did you come here, Corporal?'

'To do a deal.' Canning tried to keep his voice level, 'I want to exchange the map that one of my men stole from your friend Contin — in return for Lieutenant Waring.'

Larocque's face was expressionless, and then slowly he smiled. 'Jacques Contin isn't my friend,' he said. 'In fact, right now he isn't anybody's friend any more.' He stopped on that slightly menacing note and then said abruptly, 'We'd better sit down.'

Canning watched as the tall Belgian casually settled himself down on the dirt floor, crossing his legs and folding his arms upon his knees; and then he did likewise. Mambiro squatted distrustfully beside them, still gripping his rifle and switching his gaze from one to the other with quick, suspicious eyes.

Larocque said, 'I can talk better sitting like a native, it's become a matter of habit. Now tell me what you know about the map?'

Canning said grimly, 'I know that it pin-points the location of an unworked vein of copper that could prove to be the richest strike yet made in Katanga. And I know that you wiped out our escort and hounded the ambulance because you knew Private Baxter had stolen it from Contin. Now I'm offering it back to you in return for the girl — it's as simple as that.'

'And have you got the map with you?'

Canning smiled, 'I'm not quite that stupid. The map is hidden safely near the ambulance — you'll get it after you've escorted the Lieutenant and myself out of Sakinda.'

Larocque frowned and rubbed one hand across his lean jaw, his gaze still studying Canning's stubborn face. He said:

'What you don't seem to have realised, Corporal, is that I'm not really the king-pin around here. I plan the strategy — I teach them how to win battles and hold their rifles — but I'm still only a paid hand. Mambiro is the top dog.'

'But you *do* want that map?'

Larocque smiled somewhat bitterly in the gloom, 'I do want it, Corporal. After

346

all, it is mine. I'm a mining surveyor. I surveyed that area, discovered the copper vein and mapped the location. But I didn't tell anyone. At that time the Congo was just on the point of exploding into the present blood-bath and everyone was selling up and getting out; no one would have wanted to open up a new mine. The only sensible thing to do was to keep the whole thing a secret until the fighting had stopped and everything had simmered down, and then try to do a deal with whoever emerged as the victors. I was going to get right out of the country until the troubles had been resolved, but then I made the mistake of confiding in Contin.

'Jacques Contin was a foreman at one of the Belgian-owned mines in northern Katanga, close to where I was surveying, and he was about the nearest thing I had to a friend in this stink-heap of a country. We did a lot of drinking together, and shared the same woman. We both decided at the same time that the Congo was about to burst right open and that it was time to get out on the next plane to anywhere. We had one last celebration to say farewell and the drink made me careless enough to let slip a few hints that I had something pretty good for when things settled down again. I sobered up and found that I'd lost Contin somewhere along the line, but I didn't care much and went back to my hotel. I found Contin already there. He'd become curious about my boasting, had a look round, and found the map. And he knew enough about surveying to guess what it was all about. I was still unsteady and he cracked my head with a flower vase and bolted. There was a hell of a lot of blood and he probably thought he'd killed me. It would have been better for him if he had.'

Larocque paused and Canning said grimly:

'So you stayed on in the Congo to find him?'

'That's right. I hung about the airport at Elizabethville for a couple of days but he didn't turn up. He'd either found out that I was alive and guessed I'd be waiting for him, or else he believed

I was dead and thought the police would be looking for him. I finally found out that he'd left town but nobody knew where he'd gone. The situation was by then deteriorating rapidly and the only way for me to stay on in safety was to swear allegiance to Katanga as a white mercenary. With Contin still in the country and undoubtedly trying to find someone to whom he could sell my secret I had to stay on and guard my own interests.'

Canning was well used to the gloomy interior of the hut by now and he was constantly aware of Rona lying helplessly on the floor behind him, but there was nothing he could do to release her for the moment and he continued to face Larocque.

He said, 'I suppose that you eventually heard that Contin was in Leopoldville. But by the time you got there he had already lost the map to Baxter.'

Larocque nodded, 'Fortunately your friend Baxter left his wallet behind when he robbed Contin, and Contin passed it on to me. It was a pathetic effort to try and redeem himself which did him no good at all. However, the wallet did have Baxter's own photograph in it and that was an invaluable help. I showed the picture to every one of my gallant soldiers — or butchering terrorists, whichever you like to call them — and finally I was rewarded. One of Mambiro's men spotted Baxter here at Sakinda.'

Canning's voice became harsh and grating, 'And you massacred a whole detachment of British troops just to get at your one man. What sort of a white man are you?'

Larocque shrugged, 'You don't quite understand. You just heard Mambiro's feelings about the United Nations interfering in a black man's country. He and his warriors were determined to massacre someone anyway. If they hadn't ambushed your escort they would have tried their lovely new rifles on someone else. I simply combined our interests. I didn't particularly want to slaughter those men who were left here at the village, because I knew that the man I wanted was on board your ambulance, but there was nothing I could do to stop it.'

There was silence as Canning crushed down the savage fury that welled in his heart, and then he said at last:

'All right. I didn't come here to argue. I have the map of the mine location which you want so desperately — and you have Lieutenant Waring. Are you prepared to do a deal?'

'And what about Mambiro?'

Canning glanced into the wrinkled face of the old negro.

He said, 'He's not completely ignorant — he'll understand money. Explain how much that copper vein will be worth to anyone in a position to mine it and his black patriotism will no doubt bow before black greed.'

Larocque smiled almost sadly, 'Corporal, you still labour under a big misapprehension. A fatal misapprehension in fact. You see, the map itself means nothing. I have a copy. I could no doubt draw a thousand copies. My only purpose is to eliminate Private Baxter and anyone else who might know that the copper vein exists. And now that I know that your

351

ambulance must be hidden somewhere within walking distance on the Ningini or Kangzi roads I can send my warriors to do exactly that. I just don't need the map, and you have no bargaining position at all, Corporal — no bargaining position at all.'

The Taste of Blood

Canning knew that his gamble had failed, and failed miserably, but the stubborn streak made him keep on trying.

He said flatly, 'All right, so perhaps I don't have any bargaining position. But there's still no reason for you to go on killing. Baxter is the only one who has had any real opportunity to examine the map and he had almost forgotten that he had it. He thought that Contin was either shooting out a drunken cock-and-bull story, or else trying some hazy attempt at a confidence trick. He picked it up out of vague curiosity and I doubt if he's looked at it since, much less memorised the location of the copper vein. At the moment the map is hidden in the jungle near the ambulance and you can let it stay there and rot, or else come back with me and make sure that it's destroyed. There's no real reason why you can't allow us to just drive on.'

Larocque smiled the same sad smile, 'Corporal, you may be perfectly right. Baxter may not have realised the true value of what he was holding, and perhaps none of you could remember the details. But can you give me one logical reason why I should take such an unnecessary chance?'

Canning said desperately, 'You must have some traces of civilised decency left!'

Larocque shrugged, 'That's beside the point. Technically I'm a soldier fighting a war, and I'm on the side of the Katanga government. I'm paid to help this ragged army of mine to kill the enemy, not to let them go.'

Canning said harshly, 'What you mean is that you're determined to leave no one alive who might have seen that map. But the nurse hasn't seen it. Nobody knew that Baxter had the map until after she had been dragged back here by your men. Even if you must murder the rest of us there is still no reason why you can't let her drive on alone.'

Larocque looked as if he were about

to laugh. 'Do you really think those boys outside would let her walk out of here? They allowed you to walk in simply because they know they can cut you down any time they like and there was no need to do it right away. But neither of you could walk out. Especially the woman. They brought her here first because those were Mambiro's orders; but the only ambition some of these dark boys have is to ride a white woman, and they certainly expect to get their chance before the day is out.'

Canning felt sick inside and suddenly he knew that it was useless to argue with Larocque. Instead he turned almost despairingly to the old negro who listened in watchful silence:

'Mambiro, the woman is only a nurse, one who cares for the injured, surely you can see that nothing more can be gained by killing her. You must have some education, you can't be a complete animal.'

The thick-lipped negro face remained expressionless. Mambiro said nothing.

A sense of utter futility crawled through

Canning's stomach and he knew that Mambiro offered no hope at all. On the floor behind them Rona Waring lowered her face to the dirt and tried to hold back the nausea of horror that rose inside her. She knew that Canning was arguing in vain.

Then Larocque said flatly, 'You're wasting your time, Corporal. Another fact you seem to have forgotten is that the nurse knows my face, and she knows that I was partly responsible for the deaths of some thirty or forty U.N. troops. Surely you don't think that I'd dare let her live. At the moment nobody knows who is going to come out on top in the struggle for the Congo, but the situation must resolve itself sometime, and I'm not going to end up either shot or hanging for old war crimes.'

He smiled grimly, 'That's the way it is, Corporal. I wouldn't hand her over to the blacks if I could avoid it, but she's got to die anyway. So have you — and now I've got to organise a search for that ambulance before they get tired of waiting for you and drive on.'

He turned his head to shout to some of the warriors outside and in the same moment Canning erupted into savage, infuriated movement. Sanity told him that any effort must be futile but the stubborn streak inside him burst into homicidal violence as he swung his right fist in a crashing blow that took the unsuspecting Mambiro full in the mouth, and then he hurled himself at Larocque. His thrusting fingers fastened on the mercenary's throat to cut off the half-formed shout and they sprawled together over the hard dirt floor.

Larocque threshed frenziedly but Canning's thumbs had already sunk deep on either side of his windpipe and a hideous gurgling was the only sound that escaped from his compressed throat. The Belgian kicked, punched and clawed as they battled in gasping fury, but Canning had his chin tucked hard down to protect his own throat and was twisting his face desperately to keep the gouging fingers away from his eyes. At any moment he expected the biting thrust of a spear or the tearing kick of a bullet in his back, but still he hung on with tigerish defiance.

There was only one thought now in Canning's maddened mind, and that was to kill Larocque. There was no way in which he could save Rona or the waiting men in the ambulance, but Larocque's throat was between his crushing fingers and he must hang on until he had throttled the last dregs of life out of the writhing body beneath him.

The Belgian mercenary was the taller of the two but the stocky Corporal matched him for weight as the tempest of their movements hurled them from side to side across the gloomy interior of the hut. The single blow that Canning had spared for Mambiro had rendered the old negro totally and abruptly unconscious and once they rolled completely over his inert body as they fought. Canning was gasping for breath but Larocque's eyes were beginning to bulge and the choking rattle in his throat was a ghastly, sickening sound.

The Belgian's knee came up repeatedly into Canning's crutch but the Corporal blindly ignored every numbing, agonising blow. He ignored them as he ignored the fists that pounded at his face and the nails that clawed at his eyes. He ignored them because it didn't matter a damn if he was foully ruptured or lost an eye when at any minute he must surely die. All that mattered was to cling on to Larocque's throat and squeeze, squeeze, squeeze. As long as he could prevent the man from crying out he could yet strangle him with his bare hands.

Larocque made one last titanic effort and rolled them over again so that Canning was underneath. He pushed himself up, smashed desperately at Canning's jaw, and as the Corporal's head snapped back he locked his own fingers about the exposed throat. Canning choked in turn but he knew that he had a head start and it was still only a matter of hanging on.

Like mad dogs they struggled in near silence on the floor, each straining to strangle the other. The fury of kicking and threshing died and their bodies were almost still as they concentrated every effort into the crushing pressure of their fingers. Canning could see Larocque's eyes bulging and his tongue protruding from his gaping mouth, and then his own vision began to fade. His lungs were bursting and blackness opened its hungry maw to receive his fading senses. And then in the very last moment of fading consciousness he realised that Larocque's fingers had lost strength.

With one last effort Canning relaxed his own grip and knocked the mercenary's hands away from his throat. He rolled weakly away and lay there gasping helplessly as his senses began to return. He knew that Larocque must be dead, and that at least he had extracted some measure of vengeance for the men who had died, both Riley's men here at Sakinda and Holland's men at the stream. Now he waited for the outcry of the Bantu as they surged into the hut, and the thrusting penetration of their razor-edged spears as they exacted vengeance in their turn. He felt that he would be grateful for the first killing spear thrust when it came.

But there was no spear thrust, and no out-cry, and slowly he realised that not one of the Bantu warriors outside was aware that there was anything amiss in the hut. The whole action of the past few minutes, despite its cataclysmic ferocity, had taken place in near silence, and there had been nobody near enough to the low doorway to see into the gloom.

Slowly, feebly, Canning pushed himself to his knees. His throat was still working convulsively as he gulped for air but gradually his strength was returning. He looked at Larocque who lay with his sightless, bulging eyes staring up at the inside of the thatched roof, and there were no longer any doubts that the mercenary could be alive. The unconscious Mambiro lay a few yards away but he was weakly beginning to stir.

Canning reached his feet, swayed for a moment, and then picked up the rifle that Mambiro had dropped. He staggered towards the old negro, steadied himself, and then cracked the butt of the rifle hard against the woolly head. Mambiro became still again and Canning turned towards Rona Waring.

She was staring up at him with wide, frightened eyes, and he smiled crookedly as he moved across the hut towards her. He knelt in front of her and simply let the rifle fall, and then he took her in both arms and pulled her hard against his chest. Her cheek rested on his shoulder and her hair touched his bowed face, and he could feel the fast hammering of her heart very plainly as her bared left breast pressed against him. He touched her neck with his lips gently but for the moment there was too much emotion in him to let him speak.

At last she said huskily, 'Is — is Larocque dead?'

He pulled back from her then so that he could see her face.

'Yes,' he admitted, and his voice was almost as husky as hers had been. 'He's very, very dead.'

She had nothing else to say and he gently kissed her lips. When he drew away he said, 'I'll untie you.'

She relaxed as he lowered her to the ground and then he began to wrestle with the cords that secured her wrists. They were tight but after a few minutes he had loosened the knots enough for her to slip one hand free, and then she simply shook the cords away.

She said, 'Dear David, how did you know where to find me?'

He smiled vaguely in the half-light, 'This was the only place to start.'

'You shouldn't have come.' Her eyes were wet and her voice trembled. 'I didn't shout out when they caught me because I thought you'd come and get killed. You shouldn't have come.'

He smiled again, 'But I'm here.'

There was a dull silence and then she said, 'But they'll still kill us won't they? Larocque is dead but they'll still kill us.'

Canning couldn't answer and slowly she reached out for the rifle he had dropped. She pushed it towards him and said:

'Please, David, don't let them take me. Don't let them — don't let them touch me. I heard what Larocque said. I couldn't bear it.'

Canning knew what she was asking

363

him to do — but he wouldn't think of it. He couldn't pick up the rifle. He said clumsily, 'Rona — Rona — ' and then he pulled her into his arms again and felt sick with fear.

After a moment she stirred and reached out for the rifle. She offered it to him again and her eyes were desperate.

'Please, David. *Please*!'

Canning said savagely, 'No. No, I won't.' He thrust himself abruptly to his feet and hauled her up to face him, defiance blazed in his grey eyes again and he gripped her shoulders fiercely.

'I walked in here, Rona, and I don't see why we shouldn't just walk out. The blacks outside haven't realised that anything has gone wrong and if we simply walk through them there's just a chance that they'll think Larocque and Mambiro have granted us free passage and let us go. It's a slim chance, but at least it's a chance!'

Rona shook her head in slow despair, 'No, David. They'll never let us walk out again. Especially me. You heard what Larocque said.'

'Larocque could be wrong. And we have nothing to lose by trying.'

She hesitated, and then shook her head again. 'You have nothing to lose, David, because they'll kill you outright. But they — they'll want to rape me first. I just couldn't bear it.'

Canning gripped her shoulders harder: 'We'll walk out together and I'll take Mambiro's rifle,' he said grimly. 'And at the first sign of trouble I'll push you forward and shoot you in the back of the head. That's a promise, Rona. I won't leave you alive so that they can rape you — but I won't kill you until absolutely the last moment.'

Rona said nothing. He pushed the straying strands of her blonde hair away from her eyes and then kissed her again, still with infinite gentleness upon the lips.

'Trust me, Rona,' he begged softly. 'Please trust me. I'll do what you ask if I have to, but give me a chance to save you first.'

She looked up into his face and there was an eternity of silence before she slowly nodded her head.

Canning spared her a brief smile of gratitude, and then his mouth hardened as he picked up Mambiro's rifle in his left hand. He took her arm with his right and said grimly:

'You duck through the doorway first and I'll be right behind you. We'll walk straight across the compound and pray that nobody takes a look inside here until we've got a short start. Remember to keep looking ahead, and act as natural as you can.'

Rona swallowed hard and then nodded.

Together they crossed the hut, circling the dead body of Larocque to reach the door. Rona ducked through the low opening first and Canning followed her a second later with his hand still on her arm.

The fierce sunlight was dazzling to their eyes as they straightened up from the primeval gloom, and they hesitated for a moment in the doorway. The nearest native was a dozen yards away, but a score of eyes swivelled round to watch them as they appeared. Canning took great care to keep the rifle dragging at arm's length and completely unthreatening as he tightened his grip on Rona's shoulder and they both walked boldly forward.

The murmurings of conversation stopped again and every pair of eyes watched them with concentrated uncertainty as they walked towards the compound. There was a stiffening of black muscles as they noticed the rifle in Canning's hand, but the fact that the white man was armed now when he had arrived without weapons was just another perplexing thought and no move was made to stop him. There were almost two hundred of the silent Bantu squatting around their cooking fires, most of them in simple loin cloths but many wearing ragged shorts and vests. A few still wore the blue U.N. berets and the shreds of clothing they had scavenged in the bloody battles two days ago. Not one of them spoke, and not one of them moved, they just stared with child-like curiosity.

Canning forced down the blinding desire to glance back to see whether any of them had thought to look into the large hut in search of their leaders and walked stolidly on. He did not realise that his vicious grip was numbing and bruising Rona's shoulder as she walked slightly ahead and to one side, but he did realise that the hushed air of tense expectency could erupt into blood-lusting violence at any moment. For the Bantu needed only one taste of blood to bring them screaming to their feet with flashing spears and thrusting knives.

They reached the compound and Canning knew that the fatal moment was almost upon them. The moment when the staring natives realised that they meant to simply walk out of the village was the deciding element of time. Would they continue to gape in vague astonishment — or would they act.

Canning reached the first of the three great trees and suddenly his heart froze. Twenty yards ahead stood the young negro who had barred his path before, and this time there was no hesitation in the savage face and staring eyes. Canning remembered his promise and desperately he thrust Rona forwards. He swung the rifle up to level on her back and shoulders but the young negro had moved with fantastic speed and already his spear was arcing through the air.

The spear blade slashed across Canning's upper arm as he swayed to one side, but the force of the glancing blow spun him sideways a mere second before he could pull the trigger. Rona had stumbled forwards as he pushed her and she sprawled face down in the dust. Canning had landed on his hands and knees and the flying spear thudded into the trunk of the great tree behind him. The young Bantu uttered a whooping screech of triumph and the blood poured from the open gash in Canning's arm.

Escape From Sakinda

Complete silence greeted the young negro's single yell. He stood with his hands now resting on his hips, grinning down at Canning who balanced on his knees and one hand. Canning fought to stop himself from fainting with his misty eyes focussed on Rona as she sprawled a few yards ahead of him, and he wondered if he could still reach Mambiro's rifle that had landed just four feet away. He knew that his own death was inevitable and that at any second the electrified atmosphere must shatter as the black horde surged in for the kill, but he had promised Rona that he would not let them take her alive.

The gush of blood from his gashed arm had flowed down past his elbow and wrist and was now dripping in heavy splashes through his fingers, creating ugly red blots on the hard-packed earth. The sight of his blood was all that was needed to incite the Bantu and he pushed himself desperately to his feet. He clung to his fading senses with the tenacity of a dying bulldog, and crushed down the numbing wave of pain from his wounded left arm. The young warrior was still grinning widely, but incredibly his companions still hesitated.

Slowly Canning became aware of something new in the air. The squatting natives were watching closely but as yet making no attempt to interfere. And then slowly, very slowly, he sensed the faint suggestion of hostility in their staring eyes, and he realised that their antagonism was directed more at his enemy than at himself.

Quite suddenly he knew that the Bantu were not going to interfere. At least, not yet. For some reason there was a vague ripple of resentment towards the arrogant, glory-seeking youth. He was unpopular with his companions and for the moment they were simply waiting for the outcome.

Canning's gaze flickered towards the fallen rifle, but he knew that if he made a grab for it the silent warriors would act spontaneously. They were prepared to watch the youth go it alone, but he doubted whether they would watch him die.

The grinning negro began to advance slowly, and Canning knew that he had to do something. He turned and grasped the shaft of the spear that still bristled from the trunk of the great tree beside him and jerked it free with a quick, seesawing wrench. The oncoming negro stopped and a dozen black hands reached instinctively for their weapons. Canning let the spear blade drop harmlessly to the earth and froze. The alert warriors wavered, and then continued to merely watch.

Canning's arm was bleeding badly but iron control kept him from fainting. Rona had half turned from her prone position on the ground to stare helplessly up at him, but he ignored her and kept his own eyes fixed on the challenging negro. Suddenly he realised that there was still one faint glimmer of hope, and that was to humiliate the man. No matter how much ill-feeling there was against him the Bantu would not stand and watch one of their own number killed without retribution — but they would watch his humiliation.

The spear blade was useless because Canning knew that he dared not use it, and every moment that it remained as a threat in his hand could well incite one of the watching warriors into action. Canning kept his eyes carefully on his enemy and at the same time deliberately placed his foot on the spear just above the blade. Then with a savage, wrenching movement he snapped it off.

The Bantu stared in astonishment, and then slowly they relaxed. The white man could do no harm with a broken spear and now they could continue to watch with a clear conscience.

Canning began to move slowly forward, his eyes never leaving the negro's face. The youth was grinning again and waiting once more with his splayed hands posed arrogantly on his hips. Canning's mind raced and then he knew exactly what he had to do.

They were three paces apart and the negro's grin began to fade. Canning recognised the danger sign and knew that the youth would spring at him at any second, and even as the thought darted into his mind he lunged forward with the broken spear shaft. The young Bantu swayed expertly backwards to avoid the cracking blow that he expected to come at his head, moving his lithe body from the hips with one foot springing back to take his balance. Canning changed the direction of his one-handed blow in mid-swing and brought the spear shaft crashing down on the bare, knobbly toes of the one remaining foot.

The youth ejaculated a screech of pure agony as the bones in his toes crunched and splintered under the crushing impact, his black face became a wrinkled, tear-streaming mask of pain and he hugged his injured foot frantically as he hopped around on one leg. The watching natives uttered a titter of approval, and then when Canning swung his staff again to smack the one-legged dancer smartly across the seat of his dusty shorts the titter became a laughing howl.

Canning heard the laughter and he knew that he had won. He rapped the youth twice more across his smarting buttocks, lightly and childishly to attain the fullest humiliating effect, and then the staggering unfortunate lost his hopping balance and fell face first on to the ground. Canning threw the spear shaft away and turned to help Rona Waring to her feet, pulling her up with his one good hand.

The Bantu were laughing uproariously at the squirming antics of the yelping youth and Canning immediately propelled the half-dazed nurse towards the far side of the compound.

'Keep walking,' he said painfully. 'Just walk on again and don't look back.'

Rona obeyed, and no move was made to stop them as they crossed the compound. The grinning natives on the far side parted to let them through and some of them even cheered them on. They reached the edge of the village and the black warriors were all behind them, and then Canning felt again the numbing pain of his wounded arm. He had already lost far too much blood and he released Rona's shoulder in order to grip the gaping edges of the deep gash together. Rona steadied him and hustled him on.

They were back on the jungle road and Sakinda was behind them. They could still hear the laughter of the delighted soldier-cum-terrorists of Katanga but the sound was fading gradually away. Canning's senses were swirling in a dizzy sea of tangled greenery and dusty road that kept roaring past his face, and from time to time the worried eyes and anguished face of Rona kept intruding into the nightmare. He had the crazy feeling that someone had dipped his arm wholly into a barrel of red paint, for his arm was smothered in red, and he also knew that he had to hold the arm to stop it falling off. There was nothing else that was solid in his haze-filled mind except the occasional smudged sweetness of Rona's face and her insistent voice urging him always as 'dear David.'

Rona knew that he was on the point

of collapse, and that already his brain had succumbed to the descending wave of unconsciousness. He had lost a terrible amount of blood and it was hardly believable that he had walked clear of Sakinda before his stubborn defiance had finally begun to wane. Now she was almost fully supporting his weight and nearly frantic with worry.

She knew that at any moment the Bantu might discover the dead Larocque, or Mambiro might recover consciousness, and then the pursuit would overtake them in a matter of moments. Canning was practically helpless now as he leaned against her, and she herself was weak with fatigue from the way the Bantu had forced her through the jungle when they brought her to Sakinda. She had no idea where to find the hidden ambulance, and she doubted whether Canning's mind could now grasp enough of what was happening to be able to tell her.

Somehow she stumbled on, and somehow there was just enough stubbornness left in Canning to keep him upright with her help. They could no longer hear anything from Sakinda, which had been enveloped by the jungle behind them, and now their most pressing enemies were again the choking swirls of dust from the dirt-track road and the constant, merciless heat.

Rona felt her head swimming with exhaustion and she was almost on the point of giving up as she struggled to make a few more tottering steps. Her eyelashes were sticky with the sweat that trickled down from her temples and she was almost blind as she steered the incapable Canning. She knew that she must stop to rest; she must stop to do something for his arm and attempt to revive him before they could go on; and she looked around desperately for some break in the flanking jungle where she could drag him into hiding.

That was when she heard the sound, the mercifully familiar sound of the ambulance's engine. She stopped in the middle of the road, fully supporting Canning's dead weight, and staring along the dusty track to where the blessed miracle of the battle-scarred ambulance with its familiar bright red crosses on the white backgrounds was lumbering slowly towards her.

She waited for the vehicle to approach and blinked unbelievably as she recognised Baxter and Morris in the cab. Morris still had his arm in a sling across his chest but he was driving determinedly with one hand. The ambulance stopped exactly four feet away and then Morris clumsily descended from the cab and came forwards to help her.

'Easy, Ma'am,' he said grinning, 'We'll get him in the back.'

Together they propelled the semi-conscious Canning round to the back of the ambulance. The doors were open and a grim-faced Delayney was waiting with a ready sten gun in his hands. The Irishman hesitated, lowered his gun, and then stretched forward his arms to help the one-armed man and the nurse manoeuvre Canning inside and lay him on Baxter's blankets on the floor. Rona immediately tore up another sheet and began to fix a tourniquet on the gashed arm.

Hardman said anxiously, 'Will he be all right?'

Rona said, 'He's lost a terrible lot of blood, but I think he'll pull through.' Then she remembered the Bantu and said hurriedly, 'We must get out of here, Larocque is dead and the blacks could come after us at any minute.'

Morris gulped nervously and said, 'Yes, Ma'am.' And then he hurried back to the cab.

Rona looked towards Hardman and said weakly, 'I thought you were supposed to be hiding in the jungle somewhere.'

The big Sergeant forced a vague smile, 'That's where the Corporal left us — but after a while we took a vote and decided that we owed it to the two of you to drive a bit closer to Sakinda in case things went wrong.'

Rona said gratefully, 'Thank God you did.' And then she turned to finish tying the tourniquet as the combined efforts of Morris and Baxter reversed the ambulance in the road and they began to drive once again away from Sakinda.

They retraced their route to the fork

and then swung right along the Kangzi. They passed two more Congo villages but there were no more concentrations of terrorists and they roared through without stopping. And then, thirty-five miles from Sakinda, they ran into a determined convoy of U.N. Ghurka troops taking the long way round from Ningini to investigate the complete radio silence from Lieutenant James Holland's missing detachment.

After a terse, shocked conversation between Hardman and the officer in charge of the convoy the ambulance continued its lumbering journey to Ningini with a new escort and a fresh driver. While the column of hardened Ghurka troops continued even more determinedly towards Sakinda. The obliging officer had found Rona Waring a safety pin for her buttonless blouse before driving on, and she still tended the unconscious Canning.

Five miles later Private Garner roused himself weakly from his bed, waking fully for the first time from his still unexplained fever. He stared at the scene around him with blank, uncomprehending eyes, and then asked very plaintively if someone would please tell him what the hell was going on.

THE END

Other titles in the Linford Mystery Library

A LANCE FOR THE DEVIL
Robert Charles

The funeral service of Pope Paul VI was to be held in the great plaza before St. Peter's Cathedral in Rome, and was to be the scene of the most monstrous mass assassination of political leaders the world had ever known. Only Counter-Terror could prevent it.

IN THAT RICH EARTH
Alan Scwart

How long does it take for a human body to decay until only the bones remain? When Detective Sergeant Harry Chamberlane received news of a body, he raised exactly that question. But whose was the body? Who was to blame for the death and in what circumstances?

MURDER AS USUAL
Hugh Pentecost
A psychotic girl shot and killed Mac Crenshaw, who had come to the New England town with the advance party for Senator Farraday. Private detective David Cotter agreed that the girl was probably just a pawn in a complex game — but who had sent her on the assignment?

THE MARGIN
Ian Stuart
It is rumoured that Walkers Brewery has been selling arms to the South African army, and Graham Lorimer is asked to investigate. He meets the beautiful Shelley van Rynveld, who is dedicated to ending apartheid. When a Walkers employee is killed in a hit-and-run accident, his wife tells Graham that he's been seeing Shelly van Rynveld . . .

TOO LATE FOR THE FUNERAL
Roger Ormerod

Carol Turner, seventeen, and a mystery, is very close to a murder, and she has in her possession a weapon that could prove a number of things. But it is Elsa Mallin who suffers most before the truth of Carol Turner releases her.

NIGHT OF THE FAIR
Jay Baker

The gun was the last of the things for which Harry Judd had fought and now it was in the hands of his worst enemy, aimed at the boy he had tried to help. This was the night in which the past had to be faced again and finally understood.

PAY-OFF IN SWITZERLAND
Bill Knox

'Hot' British currency was being smuggled to Switzerland to be laundered, hidden in a safari-style convoy heading across Europe. Jonathan Gaunt, external auditor for the Queen's and Lord Treasurer's Remembrancer, went along with the safari, posing as a tourist, to get any lead he could. But sudden death trailed the convoy every kilometer to Lake Geneva.

SALVAGE JOB
Bill Knox

A storm has left the oil tanker S. S. *Craig Michael* stranded and almost blocking the only channel to the bay at Cabo Esco. Sent to investigate, marine insurance inspector Laird discovers that the Portuguese bay is hiding a powder keg of international proportions.

BOMB SCARE — FLIGHT 147
Peter Chambers

Smog delayed Flight 147, and so prevented a bomb exploding in mid-air. Walter Keane found that during the crisis he had been robbed of his jewel bag, and Mark Preston was hired to locate it without involving the police. When a murder was committed, Preston knew the stake had grown.

STAMBOUL INTRIGUE
Robert Charles

Greece and Turkey were on the brink of war, and the conflict could spell the beginning of the end for the Western defence pact of N.A.T.O. When the rumour of a plot to speed this possibility reached Counter-espionage in Whitehall, Simon Larren and Adrian Cleyton were despatched to Turkey . . .

CRACK IN THE SIDEWALK
Basil Copper

After brilliant scientist Professor Hopcroft is knocked down and killed by a car, L.A. private investigator Mike Faraday discovers that his death was murder and that differing groups are engaged in a power struggle for The Zetland Method. As Mike tries to discover what The Zetland Method is, corpses and hair-breadth escapes come thick and fast . . .

DEATH OF A MARINE
Charles Leader

When Mike M'Call found the mutilated corpse of a marine in an alleyway in Singapore, a thousand-strong marine battalion was hell-bent on revenge for their murdered comrade — and the next target for the tong gang of paid killers appeared to be M'Call himself . . .

ANYONE CAN MURDER
Freda Bream

Hubert Carson, the editorial Manager of the Herald Newspaper in Auckland, is found dead in his office. Carson's fellow employees knew that the unpopular chief reporter, Clive Yarwood, wanted Carson's job — but did he want it badly enough to kill for it?

CART BEFORE THE HEARSE
Roger Ormerod

Sometimes a case comes up backwards. When Ernest Connelly said 'I have killed . . .', he did not name the victim. So Dave Mallin and George Coe find themselves attempting to discover a body to fit the crime.

SALESMAN OF DEATH
Charles Leader

For Mike M'Call, selling guns in Detroit proves a dangerous business — from the moment of his arrival in the middle of a racial riot, to the final clash of arms between two rival groups of militant extremists.

THE FOURTH SHADOW
Robert Charles

Simon Larren merely had to ensure that the visiting President of Maraquilla remained alive during a goodwill tour of the British Crown Colony of San Quito. But there were complications. Finally, there was a Communist-inspired bid for illegal independence from British rule, backed by the evil of voodoo.

SCAVENGERS AT WAR
Charles Leader

Colonel Piet Van Velsen needed an experienced officer for his mercenary commando, and Mike M'Call became a reluctant soldier. The Latin American Republic was torn apart by revolutionary guerrilla groups — but why were the ruthless Congo veterans unleashed on a province where no guerrilla threat existed?

MENACES, MENACES
Michael Underwood

Herbert Sipson, professional black-mailer, was charged with demanding money from a bingo company. Then, a demand from the Swallow Sugar Corporation also bore all the hallmarks of a Sipson scheme. But it arrived on the opening day of Herbert's Old Bailey trial — so how could he have been responsible?

MURDER WITH MALICE
Nicholas Blake

At the Wonderland holiday camp, someone calling himself The Mad Hatter is carrying out strange practical jokes that are turning increasingly malicious. Private Investigator Nigel Strangeways follows the Mad Hatter's trail and finally manages to make sense of the mayhem.

THE LONG NIGHT
Hartley Howard

Glenn Bowman is awakened by the 'phone ringing in the early hours of the morning and a woman he does not know invites him over to her apartment. When she tells him she wishes she was dead, he decides he ought to go and talk to her. It is a decision he is to bitterly regret when he finds himself involved in a case of murder . . .

THE LONELY PLACE
Basil Copper

The laconic L.A. private investigator Mike Faraday is hired to discover who is behind the death-threats to millionaire ex-silent movie star Francis Bolivar. Faraday finds a strange state of affairs at Bolivar's Gothic mansion, leading to a horrifying mass slaughter when a chauffeur goes berserk.

THE DARK MIRROR
Basil Copper

Californian private eye Mike Faraday reckons the case is routine, until a silenced gun cuts down Horvis the antique dealer and involves Mike in a trail of violence and murder.

DEADLY NIGHTCAP
Harry Carmichael

Mrs. Esther Payne was a very unpopular lady — right up to the night when she took two sleeping tablets and died. Traces of strychnine were discovered in the tube of pills, but only four people had the opportunity to obtain the poison for Esther's deadly night-cap . . .

DARK DESIGN
Freda Hurt

Caroline Lane missed her husband when he was away on his frequent business trips — until the mysterious phone-call that introduced Neil Fuller into her life. Then came doubts that led her to question her husband's real whereabouts, even his identity.

ESCAPE A KILLER
Judson Philips

Blinded by an acid-throwing fanatic, famous newspaperman Max Richmond moved to an isolated mansion in Connecticut. On a visit there, Peter Styles, a writer for NEWSVIEW MAGAZINE, became involved in a diabolical plot. The trap was not meant for him, but he was as helpless as the intended victim.

LONG RANGE DESERTER
David Bingley

Jack Walmer deserts from the French Foreign Legion to fight with a British Unit. Time and again, Jack must prove his allegiance by risking his life to save British servicemen. His final task is an attack on an Italian fortress, where the identity of a British prisoner holds the key to his future happiness.